Clara's Mourning

J. Willis Sanders

ISBN: 978-1-954763-51-7 (paperback)
ISBN: 978-1-954763-50-0 (ebook)

BUGGS ISLAND BOOKS

Printed in the United States of America
Cover art by BookCoverZone.com

Verified Amazon reviews for *The Colors of Eliza Gray*

"Captivating! … J. Willis Sanders has captured love in this story. Love of a father to his daughter, love between brothers and sisters, and true love struggling to find a way to a future together. I look forward to Sanders' next book."

"I can honestly say that "The Colors of Eliza Gray" had me hooked from chapter one! It had me wishing for a "happily ever after" for Eliza from the beginning. Every emotion is found in this book and J. Willis Sanders definitely knows how to draw his readers in! I had read half of it before I realized it and finished it up the next morning!"

"Enjoyed this book so much! Stayed up way past my bedtime to finish it. Romantic and inspiring story. Great descriptions enabling the reader to visualize the scenes. Highly recommended."

"You won't be able to put this awesome book down! Love, love of a father and their love!!!! Please write another about how their lives are going!!!"

"The Colors of Eliza Gray is one of the most compelling books I've ever read. Beginning with a hearing-impaired abused Eliza. Taking you through her education and life altering experiences once she has her world opened to her. I truly hated it to end. Can't wait for the next book."

By J. Willis Sanders

The Eliza Gray Series
The Colors of Eliza Gray
The Colors of Denver Andrews
The Colors of Tess Gray

The Outer Banks of North Carolina Series
The Diary of Carlo Cipriani
If the Sunrise Forgets Tomorrow
Love, Jake

The Hope Series
The Coincidence of Hope
The Yearning of Hope
The Gift of Hope

The Clara Engelman Series
Clara's Mourning
Coming soon, *Clara's Courtship*

The Forgiveness Quilt: An Amish Christmas Carol

The Essence of Emmaline Strong

Writing as J. D. James
Reid Stone: Hard as Stone
Reid Stone: Red Rage

Readers: please enjoy the first chapter of *Clara's Courtship* at end of this book.
Also included are the first chapters of *The Colors of Eliza Gray* and *The Essence of Emmaline Strong*.
Thank you for reading,
J. Willis Sanders

Dear readers,

The main character in this book is a young Beachy Amish Mennonite woman. There are many different Amish orders. One reason I chose this order is because they can use any technology except radios and television, which can lead to some interesting plot devices such as using cell phones and driving vehicles. A quick internet search of the Beachy Amish Mennonites shows why they don't use TV or radios, as well as the general rules they follow, also known as their Ordnung, which can vary greatly from community to community like with most Amish Ordnungs. Interestingly, according to research, they also don't speak Pennsylvania Dutch like most Amish do.

Although this book is fiction, I tried to write it accurately by researching it online and asking questions on online forums. Yes, all Amish value faith, family, and community, but I think we can be sure that life's challenges, just like anyone else's challenges, can cause turmoil in their lives.

The Amish and Mennonites are interesting people with admirable work ethics and dedication to God, and I enjoy writing about them in such a way as to make them have human frailties like the rest of us.

After all, a good story includes conflicts like we all have. Since many of those conflicts happen when we search for someone to love, it's likely the Amish and Mennonites may experience the same thing depending on the individual and the circumstances, which is where the magic of fiction takes over. Yes, I'm smiling, because I dearly love the magic of fiction.

Also, if you've read my Eliza Gray series, you'll recognize some of the side characters in this book from that series. No doubt some readers of the series would like to get glimpses of their lives after the series ended, so this is why I chose to include them, as well as my hometown of Clarksville, Virginia, and the surrounding counties of Charlotte and Halifax and the town of South Boston.

If you'd like to visit a great website about the Beachy Amish Mennonites, here's the link: http://www.beachyam.org/

If you'd like to visit Clarksville online to learn about it and Kerr Lake, what us locals call Buggs Island Lake, visit https://clarksvilleva.com/#/

Thank you for reading,
J. Willis Sanders

Clara's Mourning

Chapter 1

Torn between admiration for the sunrise and the need to keep her memories of Abram tucked away like a chaste kiss, Clara didn't know whether to smile or cry. She had enjoyed similar scenes with him after they were married, but the one before her, nor the ones to come, would never compare. Still, the beauty of the breaking day was a gift from God, and it was worthy of her attention.

The shimmering line of crimson above the horizon lit the distant treetops with flame. The first air of dawn stirred, cold and brisk. In the chicken coop behind the barn, the rooster crowed. In the maple tree beside the single-story home clothed with white-painted boards, two bluebirds left their house attached to the trunk and fluttered to a limb to warble their waking song.

Clara's footsteps crunched in the greening grass. Her breath plumed before her face and dissipated as it shrouded her cheeks with white. She entered the dark kitchen and left the basket of eggs and the still illuminated flashlight on the table to light her way. For a moment she considered checking on Edna and John but didn't. Her footsteps, no matter how soft, might wake them if she approached their room, and they needed all the sleep they could get.

She paused for water. At the sink, sipping from the glass, she leaned closer to the window. Over the hill between her farm and the neighbor's farm, the rising sun etched the first rays of yellow into the sky. It was the first of April in southern Virginia, still capable of frost, and she had forgotten her mittens while gathering eggs, leaving her hands chilly from the morning cold.

She finished the water and went to the cookstove to add wood to the glowing embers. Leaving the cast iron door open, she pulled a chair over from the table and sat to warm her hands near the opening.

How she missed Abram's warm embraces in the nights, now long and lonely after his funeral a month ago. His death had left a hole in her life like a well without water: cold and damp, without the least bit of comfort. Four-year-old Edna and three-year-old John missed their papa as well, evidenced by the nightmares that still woke them at least three times a week. Thankfully, they had slept the last two nights without crying, nor asking when he would return from that terrible dark hole in the earth, now filled beneath the old oak tree behind the house.

Although she and Abram had been teaching them about their Heavenly home, they were too young to understand, much less understand about death. Regardless, Clara had tried to explain how living things died, using the example of a hen that had died of old age a few days after the funeral. All the children had managed was to look at her with huge, questioning eyes rimmed with tears.

The rooster crowed again, followed by more of the bluebird's warbling entering the screened door. She had left the wooden door open to remind her to milk the cow, one of the many chores that were now left to her alone.

Tears threatened. She attempted to blink them away.

Not only was she forced to endure life without Abram's love, she was forced to try to keep the farm profitable enough to feed her family and pay the bills.

Clara palmed the wetness from her eyes. How could she do all that without help? Not only had she never hitched the plow to their used tractor, she didn't know how to drive it, much less how to maintain it. At least she had two seasons of vegetables canned, so she and the children had plenty to eat, and the chickens would provide eggs and meat.

She bowed her head in prayer to thank her Beachy Amish Mennonite brothers and sisters, who had built the coffin and helped with the funeral, and with bringing enough food so cooking hadn't been necessary for a week. She also appreciated their vows to continue helping, including with money, but it felt wrong to Clara to not earn her own way.

Even Bishop Silverman had calmed the children by saying all would be well, that their papa would never stop watching over them. If only Clara could've been comforted by those words. Abram loved her needlework, so she had sewn a collar of white lace to her black dress in hopes of honoring him with her precious memories. Instead, as she fingered the lace during the funeral, all she could do was weep. Although the women in her community were allowed to wear small feminine adornments and to braid their hair when they pinned it at the nape of their necks, she wished she had left the dress plain.

Looking for a new area with large acreage for sale, plus being frugal with their meager funds, she and Abram had bought this farm. Tucked away in a somewhat isolated area in Charlotte County, it was a late wedding gift to each other with the money his and her parents had given them. Unfortunately, her and Abram's parents lived in Pennsylvania, where their other children lived. Yes, they had made the drive for the funeral, but they had returned shortly after, saying they were needed back home.

Noting how the wood wasn't catching fire in the embers, Clara adjusted it with a poker until it flamed.

The smell of woodsmoke brought back the memory of her and Abram's first night here together, snug in several quilts in front of this very woodstove, its door open on a freezing January evening. Although they slept that way when it was bitterly cold, it was an adventure too, enjoyed in the early days of their marriage.

After closing the stove door, she got the milk pail. She considered the mittens on the shelf above the coat rack, but she wouldn't be able to roll her fingers properly as she milked, and the cow sometimes kicked if she felt something different.

Clara paused for another swallow of water. In the window over the sink, her reflection stared back. She'd risen and put on Abram's pants and wide-brimmed hat, both warmer than her dress and the bandana she tied over her hair while she worked. She'd also put on two pair of his socks and his work boots, leaving her looking nothing like the proper Beachy Amish housewife. Then again, the farm was over twenty miles away from the community she belonged to, a newer one north of the present one in Nathalie, Virginia, in Halifax County, so she wouldn't be caught out of her traditional clothing. Even if she were, she had arrived at the point of not caring, which she *didn't* care for.

Then again, she knew God loved her regardless, and His acceptance was more important than what others thought. Also, maybe she wore Abram's clothes to recall his warmth surrounding her, like a second skin of love she would never shed.

The two bluebirds continued to warble, and the sound saddened her. She and Abram used to call their nightly talks in bed "talking like the bluebirds," when they spoke of the children and their dreams for them.

Clara refused to judge other religious beliefs, but she was grateful for her and Abram's Beachy Amish Mennonite Ordnung. Still, although a used pickup truck sat by the barn, she didn't know how to drive it. They had also discussed getting a telephone when they could afford it, which they couldn't yet. They hadn't minded living simply until they could do better, but how some of the stricter Amish lived without conveniences such as indoor plumbing, Clara didn't know. She, however, admired their strength in doing so.

Peering at her reflection in the window again, she tucked several strands of her red hair, having escaped their pins, inside the bandana beneath Abram's hat. She then drank another swallow of water and took the flashlight and pail to the barn to milk the cow.

Inside the two-story structure, where the aroma of hay and manure permeated the crisp air, she sat on a stool beside the cow and rubbed her hands together to warm them. Few things angered Clara like having the cow kick the pail over from cold hands.

With her palms warm, she began milking. As the metallic rhythm of the twin streams struck the side of the pail, Clara grew drowsy. She once loved the misty feeling of sitting in the quiet of the barn while listening to Abram milking the cow. Although their Ordnung allowed many modern conveniences, they preferred growing their own food and having fresh milk for butter and cheese, which they sold from a stand near the mailbox when they had extra. They had bought the house from an Amish family who belonged to a stricter Ordnung. Abram had planned to have the entire home wired when he hired a man to install the electric pump for the indoor plumbing. Instead, the money was needed to repair their old pickup truck, to repair the barn's roof, and to build a pig pen and a place for them to shelter when it rained and snowed. Unfortunately, Abram had fallen from the loft and broken his neck. Yes, they had spent the money on everything except the pigs, and Clara was glad. She didn't think she could kill and butcher one without Abram's help.

The cow mooed, jarring her from her thoughts. Outside, gravel crunched in the driveway. She knew only one person in this area, so it might be the neighbor arriving in his pickup truck. Standing, Clara girded herself for a confrontation.

Jonah Ellis was one of those men who refused to believe women were equal to men. Two weeks ago, when she, Edna, and John had stopped to rest on their walk from the local market about five miles away, Mr. Ellis had come along and stopped to insist he give them a ride home. Yes, his idea was practical, but the way he looked down at her from what was likely his six-foot plus height—she being a petite five-foot four inches and as slender as a newborn whitetail fawn—had angered her. It also hadn't helped that he wasn't Amish or Mennonite, or that his honey-brown eyes seemed to pluck her nerves, or that his wavy brown hair like Abram's had caught her eye, or that he lived with the woman he was engaged to. To Clara, aside from it being a sin, living together out of wedlock was like the English saying: "Why buy the cow when you can get the milk for free?"

The vehicle door slammed. Heavy footsteps thudded up the steps and across the porch. Hard knuckles knocked on the screened door. "Mrs. Engelman? It's Bishop Silverman."

Panic struck a harsh chord inside Clara's chest. Despite not caring what others thought of her wearing Abram's clothes, she didn't know what the bishop might say. More strands of her red hair hung from beneath Abram's hat. She tucked them in, made sure the zipper of his huge canvas coat was up, and left the barn.

As Abram's heavy boots clomped in the gravel, the bishop, about to knock on the door again, turned. "Clara?"

Not only did his look of disapproval slow Clara's stride, him calling her by her first name for the first time did as well. "I was milking the cow,

Bishop Silverman." She wrapped her arms around herself. "It's very cold. That's why I'm wearing Abram's things."

A single twitch in the bishop's cheek showed his further disapproval. "I … well, I suppose you need to be warm."

Clara moved closer. Her breath, hard and fast, jetted from her nostrils in twin streams, the same as from the bishop's. "I would offer coffee," she said. "The children are still asleep and I hate to wake them."

"I understand. How are you— I mean, how are they doing?" His eyes darted to one side.

Unless Clara missed her guess, the bishop was here for an unwelcome reason—one that her best friend, Alison Henley, had suggested he might attempt. Before Clara and Abram moved here, so Alison had said, the bishop's wife had left him and filed for divorce a year later. Clara had never heard of such a thing in an Amish or Mennonite community, so she wasn't sure if he could marry again. Regardless, she wasn't ready for that—if ever—and certainly not to Bishop Silverman.

The bishop cleared his throat. His face was red, either from the cold or embarrassment. He came closer. His hand raised to Clara's temple, where a single fingertip touched her skin. "I don't know how, but I never realized you have red hair." He licked his lips. "I came to ask—"

Clara backed away. "As you can see, I'm very busy."

"Do you need help with anything?"

"No, please. Why did you come?"

"I … well …"

Clara could see his intention in the way his eyes focused on hers. With Abram gone, the bishop had come to hover over her like a hawk seeking a mouse in the field of her mourning.

He raised his hand to her temple again. She wanted to run, to scream, to grab the pitchfork from the barn and make him leave. Instead, she simply stood there. If not, if he went back home and spread the word that he had caught her out of her dress and kapp, who knew what would happen.

The bishop withdrew his hand without touching her. "You have straw in your hair. I was only going to take it out."

Clara brushed at her hair; a piece of straw fell at her feet.

The bishop went to his pickup and returned with a huge pot covered with a lid. "This is cabbage soup I made last night. I enjoy cooking but I made too much, likely because I was thinking of my … well, Sarah's gone, but I can't stop thinking about her. I'm sure you feel the same way about Abram."

Shame heated Clara's cheeks. This poor man missed his wife as much as she missed Abram, and he was only trying to help in any way he could. She took the pot. "Thank you for thinking of the children and me."

"You're welcome." He shoved his hands into his pants pockets. "You're right, it's very cold this morning."

Clara gave him the pot. "Please take that to the kitchen table while I get the milk. I'll make coffee to warm us up."

He took the pot. "I've been thinking about your situation here. You can't drive, and you live far away from our community." He paused. "You have a good neighbor in Jonah. I know him well and trust him. I'm sure he's willing to help around the farm if you need him."

Clara nodded. She could use help now and then, and it was kind of the bishop to make allowances for her situation by suggesting her neighbor. Maybe she had misjudged Mr. Ellis when he had offered to give her and the children a ride.

She took the milk to the kitchen. Beside the table, the bishop faced her. "You said Edna and John are still asleep?"

Filling the percolator with water, Clara looked over her shoulder. "They still have nightmares about the funeral. Anytime they go near a hole outside, no matter how small, they run from it. I tried to explain death to them and how they'll see their papa again, but they're too young to understand."

"Would you like me to try?" the bishop asked.

Clara noted the sincerity in his voice. "I'd rather not until they're older. They're starting to sleep better now." She finished filling the percolator, measured coffee, and took it to the stove.

Along with noting the bishop's sincere voice, she also noted the hint of gray hair at his temples, plus how he hadn't removed his wide-brimmed hat, black as a crow's breast feathers. She took Abram's coat and hat to the hanger and returned to the stove, rubbing her cold hands together over the hot metal.

The bishop took her cue and hung his coat and hat on the peg beside hers, which caused a twinge of anger in her. It was as if he had taken Abram's place without asking, and she didn't like it at all. Despite her warming hands, she continued rubbing them together. Although the bishop seemed nice, she had the feeling he was watching her, possibly thinking of her as his future wife even now. Fear prickled along the back of her neck.

"Mrs. Engelman?"

Clara refused to turn. At least he had called her

by her married name. "Yes?"

"If I'm making you uncomfortable by being here, I can leave."

His voice was soft and gentle. Shame heated Clara's cheeks again. Perhaps she was oversensitive because of losing Abram. She turned to face the patient man. "I admit it's strange having another man here with Abram gone." She paused to give her confused mind time to find the right words. "I realize you're my bishop, but …" Her hands began to tremble. She raised them to her face and spun away to cry.

If her feelings about the bishop wanting her for a wife were true, she expected him to approach her, to touch her, perhaps to place a hand on her shoulder, but none of that happened.

Behind her, his footsteps shuffled on the hardwood floor. His clothing rustled as he donned his coat. More footsteps followed. The screened door softly closed, and the gravel crunched beneath his vehicle's tires as he drove away.

Clara sank to her knees. Sobs continued to wrack her body until she had to force herself to stop or risk having a sore throat. Also, she needed to wake Edna and John soon, and she didn't want a raspy voice and reddened eyes to betray her tears.

She stood to the sound of percolating coffee. The aroma rose in the steam coming from the spout, reminding her of Abram again. He loved breakfast, particularly coffee. A pang of sorrow hit again, and Clara's sobs returned.

As much as she loved her sweet and gentle husband, how long would it take until she could treasure her memories of him with joy instead heartache?

Chapter 2

A month after the bishop had brought the cabbage soup, Clara didn't know what to do with the pot. He lived near their community, too far to walk. At least he hadn't returned for it, which must've meant he knew he had upset her. As she considered that day's interaction, guilt hounded her for not attending church the past two months, whenever her community met in Alison's or someone else's home. She felt the guilt deeply, but she couldn't go anywhere far away until she learned how to drive.

In the yard staring at the truck, Clara considered the last few days. Although the children continued to sleep without nightmares, she had begun to have them. Words couldn't describe how much she missed Abram. In her dreams, however, he told her of his wishes for her to be happy without him, that he would always love her no matter what. Then the nightmare portion would strike, with him laughing at her because she knew so little of the work he did on their farm. He had never done that, of course, but the nightmares' realism never failed to jerk her up from her pillow with a scream about to erupt from the depths of her soul.

Shaking her head, she realized she needed to plow the garden spot. With Edna and John at her side, she went to the plow to the right of the barn to study it. She had watched Abram plow but had never watched him hitch it to the tractor.

She shook her head again at her lack of knowledge. Why hadn't she asked him to show her more? She stopped shaking her head. She knew why, because neither of them had planned on him dying in his mid-twenties, in the prime of his life.

Edna touched one of the plow's blades. "It's the plow, Mama."

John tapped the blade with the toe of his leather shoe. "It's dirty."

Instead of tapping it with her shoe, Clara considered kicking it. She was an intelligent woman; she should be able to figure it out. Maybe the stress of losing Abram and needing to depend on herself for everything was making her doubt her abilities.

In the road to their right, a vehicle engine rumbled and slowed. The neighbor pulled his huge diesel, dual-wheeled pickup into the driveway and parked beside the house.

Beaming a grin, Jonah Ellis, wearing faded blue jeans, work boots, and a long-sleeved blue shirt, his brown hair ruffled by the breeze, shut the pickup door and waved.

To be polite, Clara attempted a weak smile. Edna and John faced the man. "He wanted to give us a ride that day," Edna said.

Mr. Ellis neared them. "I didn't introduce myself either, young lady." He knelt to look her in the eye. "I'm Mr. Ellis. You can call me Jonah."

Edna glanced at Clara and returned to Mr. Ellis. "Like in the whale?"

Ellis laughed. "Not me, but I saw a whale at the beach one time."

John's eyes squinted. "Beach?"

Standing, Ellis groaned. "Whew, my back is giving me a fit from hoeing weeds in my garden." He took a phone from its holder on his belt. Clara watched as he swiped the screen until a photo of a beach and the ocean appeared. "I love the beach but Lydia hates it." He lowered the screen so Edna and John could see. "There you go. That's a beach and the ocean."

John touched the screen. "Blue water."

"Where's the whale?" Edna asked.

"I didn't have my phone that day," Ellis said as he stood. He showed the photo to Clara. "Have you ever been to the beach, Mrs. Engelman? If you haven't, you really should go sometime."

Why, so I can get out of my Mennonite rut? hovered on Clara's lips. Still, she had to admit to the beauty of the blue-green waves capped with foam, their white-bearded chins ready to tip toward the sand. She looked away from the phone. "Can I help you with something, Mr. Ellis?"

"Jonah, please." He tousled John's hair, brown like Abram's had been. "Can I ask your children's names? They sure are cute."

"I'm very busy."

"I saw that from the road. Do you need help with your—" Ellis's mouth hung open. "I'm sorry about your husband. I was out of town with Lydia during the funeral. I can't imagine what you're going through." He glanced at the children, who were kneeling to pick a dandelion and blow its thistles, then returned to Clara. "I was going to ask if you need help with your garden. I'd be glad to plow it with my tractor. It would only take a few minutes."

The kindness in Ellis's eyes surprised Clara. Like she had thought earlier, perhaps she had misjudged him, although his living out of wedlock with his fiancé still bothered her. "Thank you for the offer, but I need to get accustomed to doing things on my own."

"I don't mind," Ellis said. "I introduced myself to your husband in town once. He told me how he wanted to wire your home and barn for electricity, but didn't have the money at the time. I got my electrical license a few years back but decided to buy a farm. Lydia thinks raising beef cattle is a good idea. Well, she thinks it'll make us wealthy. I still do electrical work, but I love working in my garden." Ellis shared a slight grin. "She doesn't care for gardening much. I have a feeling she won't like raising cattle when we ever get around to it."

To Clara, Ellis's revelations about Lydia didn't make them a good match. He was a bit taller than Abram, handsome in a rugged sort of way. She paused her thoughts. Abram had never mentioned talking with their neighbors. In fact, he had never mentioned them at all, or how they lived together out of wedlock. She thought they both shared the same religious convictions. Could his have not been as firm as hers?

She told the children to stand and took their hands. "I really am busy, Mr.—"

"Jonah, remember? If it helps, you can think of me as the man in the whale."

"In his belly," Edna said. "Mama taught me that."

"In the Bible, right?"

Edna nodded, and Jonah faced Clara again. "The Amish and Mennonites have always intrigued me. Despite Lydia's attempted influence, I'm a simple man at heart. I've been to different churches off and on since I left home, but I can't seem to find one I'd like to join." He paused. "Maybe that's because I haven't studied the Bible much. I've tried, but the meaning escapes me."

Edna patted his hand. "Mama could teach you like she teached me."

Despite Mr. Ellis's presence, Clara laughed at Edna's "teached." "You mean 'teaches,' honey."

Ignoring Clara, Edna picked another dandelion and blew the thistles.

Jonah, who was watching her, faced Clara. "You're the first Amish parent I've heard call their child a name like 'honey.' Is there a reason for that?"

"Abram and I are … were … well, I'm a Beachy Amish Mennonite. I'm not sure, but we probably have the most relaxed Ordnung. We also use most any technology except for radios and television. We consider them an intrusion of the outside world into the home."

"I'm not fond of what's on TV these days myself," Jonah said. "I'll take a good book over that anytime."

The remark tempted Clara to laugh. "Not Amish novels, I hope. I was selling tomatoes one day from the stand by the mailbox, and a women went on and on about reading Amish novels and how she loved the lifestyle. Apparently, she didn't know the difference between Amish fact and Amish fiction. We work much harder than most people know."

"I like the large families," Jonah said, glancing at the children, but a couple would be fine with me. I hope to have a family like yours one day." He faced Clara again. "My mom had red hair like yours."

Clara couldn't help herself. "You said 'had?'"

"She and Dad divorced the year I turned eighteen, and it kind of feels like they died. I don't have any brothers or sisters. Mom and dad were great to me, although I don't see her often. She remarried and moved to California. Dad died from a heart attack the following year, and he made sure to take care of my needs with a good life insurance policy. I sure miss him. Money isn't everything."

Almost on its own, Clara's fingertips raised toward his sleeve but stopped just short of touching it. "I'm ..." She swallowed. "I'm sorry. As you know, I'm aware of how it feels to lose a loved one, Mr. Ellis."

Regardless of the sadness of the moment, Jonah smiled. "Just what must I do to have you call me Jonah?"

"Well …" Clara said, indecision tightening her throat.

Jonah knelt by Edna and John. "What do you think? Should your mama call me Jonah or Mr. Ellis?"

"I like Jonah," Edna said.

"Jonah!" John squealed.

He stood. "How about it, Mrs. Engel—I mean, Clara. Will you call me Jonah? If not, I'll hold you down and let these two cuties of yours tickle you until you agree."

Edna and John looked up at her expectantly. Jonah leaned over so Clara would be looking into his eyes instead of theirs. "Hey, I'm right here." He straightened. "How about it? I'll even trade you some electrical work and plowing your garden for teaching me about the Bible."

"Good," Edna said. "Mama can't drive Papa's tractor."

"No?" Jonah asked. "Maybe I can teach her how."

Clara considered his request. She wasn't sure about his offer of trading work for her teaching him about the Bible, but leading someone to the miracle of God's word was a worthy goal, even if it meant calling him by his first name. Also, if he helped with the electricity, the garden, and teaching her how to drive the tractor, she could plant the garden and can food to restock the shelves and cabinets in the kitchen. About to accept his offer, she hesitated. Some of the people in her community might think being friends with another man so soon after losing Abram was wrong, especially an English man. Since that was the case, it was a good thing they rarely came to see her. Even Bishop Silverman hadn't come since the last time, a month ago. Clara didn't know why, but regardless of his understanding her sobbing and leaving when he was here, she felt a twinge of resentment against him. Then again, he hadn't pressed her about returning to the worship services she had been skipping since Abram died. After all, it wasn't like she could drive there. The man had his good points too, such as bringing the cabbage soup. Clara decided to clear her thoughts and return to Jonah, who was waiting patiently for her answer.

"Very well, Mr. Ellis. Jonah it is."

Chapter 3

Three days later, perspiring in the heat of the afternoon, Clara watched Jonah plow the garden. When the dark sod was turned and the rows were formed, she brought him a glass of lemonade from the kitchen. In the driveway, the tractor's rumble ended. Jonah climbed off, wiped beads of sweat from his forehead with his sleeve, and joined Clara in the shade of the maple. "Ah, I see you like lemonade, Clara."

She offered the glass. "I brought it for you."

He waved the glass away. "I'll have a beer when I get home."

Sipping the lemonade, Clara made a mental checkmark about the negative of Jonah drinking alcohol.

As she lowered the glass, he took it and drank anyway, even turning it so his lips pressed the glass where hers had pressed. Although the simple but complicated gesture puzzled her, it also sent a pang of wonder through her about why he had done it. Was he attracted to her and wanted to show it? Crossing her arms, she pinched herself. What a ridiculous thought, carnal and unbidden. How could she think such a thing? Abram was the love of her life. No other man would ever replace him, especially not one who lived with another woman without marriage vows, let alone one who wasn't Beachy Amish Mennonite.

Jonah drank again, this time swallowing half of the lemonade. Licking his lips, he offered the glass, making sure to turn the side he had drank from toward her. "Go ahead, I'm not poisonous."

She took the glass and emptied it into the grass. Over their heads in the tree, the bluebird pair warbled, drawing Clara's attention to something other than thinking about how Jonah might be attracted to her.

He pulled out his shirttail, which revealed firm stomach muscles. "I've never met Alison," he said. "It was nice of her to take the children while we work on the garden."

Clara said nothing. Yes, she had told Alison she wanted to work on the garden, but she hadn't mentioned anything about Jonah. Alison had also been kind enough to keep them for the night, which would allow her to take Edna and John to tomorrow's worship service for the first time since Abram had died. Of course, they wanted to play with Alison's children too.

A sudden question rose in Clara's mind. Having turned away to empty the glass, she faced Jonah again. "Does Lydia mind you coming here?"

Jonah looked up into the tree. "I love to listen to the bluebirds sing."

"Jonah?"

"Are you happy with the garden?" he asked, still looking into the tree. "I can make it bigger if you want." He kept peering into the tree. "I need to teach you how to drive the tractor too."

"Jonah?"

He faced her. "When can I start wiring the house for lights?" He snapped his fingers. "That's right. I plowed your garden, so you owe me a Bible lesson. We have to keep our relationship strictly business, right?"

A twinge of anger made Clara clench her teeth. "You didn't answer me about Lydia."

"What about her?"

"What do you mean, 'what about her?' I just asked you."

With the hint of a grin, Jonah looked up into the tree again. "You sure are easy to tease."

Clara placed her hands on her hips, the same as if she were admonishing Abram during one of their rare disagreements. "I'm trying to be serious, Jonah. What does Lydia—"

He lowered his eyes to look into hers. "I heard you the first time, Clara. Lydia and I trust each other completely. Besides, you're Beachy Amish Mennonite and I'm not. I don't plan to join your community to be with you and you don't plan to leave it to be with me, right?"

Clara's mouth hung open. What a frustrating man.

He leaned down from his height advantage to look her in the eye. "Is it against your Ordnung for an English man to tell an Amish woman how attractive she is?"

Heat filled Clara's cheeks. Jonah's lips pursed into a grin. "That blush is beautiful too, but I didn't mean I was going to tell you how attractive *you* are. You're really quite plain." His eyes focused upward for a second. "That white kapp with your hair pinned under it doesn't do a thing for you." He touched the sleeve of her sky-blue dress with a fingertip. "The dress is okay. It's not as loose fitting as on some of the other Mennonite women I see in South Boston." He tapped the toe of his work boot to her bare foot. "Do you ever wash your feet? They sure are slender. They might be your most endearing quality, except I'm sure they smell worse than mine in my boots."

Clara pointed at his stomach. "Well, your most endearing quality is that flabby belly of yours."

Jonah patted his stomach. "Yeah, Lydia tells me I need to lose a few pounds."

Shaking her head, Clara didn't know whether to laugh or pout. "You *do* need a Bible lesson. You joke too much. Are you telling the truth about Lydia?"

Jonah leaned his back against the tree. "Oh, she knows she has me wrapped around her little finger." He checked his watch. "What if I drive to South Boston for a pizza and you give me a Bible lesson after? Lydia's visiting relatives in Ohio, and I hate to eat alone."

Clara considered his request. Some members of her community did accept visitors into their homes. Besides, if anyone needed a lesson from the Bible, such as how to be humble, Jonah did. Also, since the bishop had allowed her and Jonah to be alone while he helped with the garden, teaching him the Bible alone should be fine as well. "Fine," she said, toning her voice as if he were a child. "But you need to promise to behave first."

Jonah left for his tractor. "I'll take this home and shower first. See you in a bit."

Clara took the glass to the kitchen counter, got

more ice from the ice box, and poured more lemonade. Along with their plans to buy a new truck, she and Abram had dreamed of a refrigerator. She didn't mind Jonah plowing the garden, but she preferred to not allow him to wire the house like he had mentioned. For one thing, he would be with her and the children during the work, and as much as Edna and John had enjoyed the few minutes they had spent with him on the day they had met, she didn't want them to get attached to him. She drank the cold, refreshing lemonade. But having a refrigerator and freezer, where she could make her own ice without buying it to keep the ice box cold, would be amazing.

As she raised the glass again, she caught a whiff of underarm odor and decided to bathe. She didn't think her feet smelled as bad as Jonah's in his boots, but the dirt on the outsides, plus the grass stains on the soles, etched her skin like brown and green spider webs.

While a bucket of water warmed on the woodstove, she undressed in her room. She didn't admire her slender body like Abram had, who had called her his "Little Bluebird" because of her skinny legs. Still, she'd rather eat sensibly. After all, gluttony was a sin.

She took the water to the bathroom, warmed more and brought more until the tub was full. Yes, they had indoor plumbing and a bathroom with a tub, but without electricity and a hot water heater, it was a chore to heat buckets of water and tote them back and forth. The tub was another of her and Abram's plans gone awry.

She sank into the warm water and scrubbed herself. When the water turned a dingy shade of brown, she repeated the process with clean water, then washed her hair, toweled it as dry as possible, and pinned it up again. Dressed in a clean, blue dress, she rinsed the brown ring from inside the tub.

Outside, the diesel engine of Jonah's truck rumbled to a stop. As she entered the kitchen to unlock the door, she realized she had forgotten her kapp. The truck door slammed. Jonah knocked on the door. "The pizza man is here, Clara. Open up before it gets cold."

Clara had once smelled a frozen pizza that Alison had cooked. Not caring to impose on the family's dinner despite the delicious aroma of roasted bell peppers, onions, tomatoes, and sausage, she could only imagine the taste. Now it was right outside her door. Run back to her room for the kapp or not? Her Ordnung said to do so, but her watering mouth said she could let Jonah in first, which was also the polite thing to do. She opened the door and held it for him. "That didn't take long."

He set the huge, flat box on the table. "That's because I know how to drive. We'll have to schedule your lessons for your truck and the tractor."

Clara got two plates from the cupboard. As she took them to the table, one of her damp feet slipped on the hardwood floor. Although Jonah grabbed her arm to steady her, her hair, damp and heavy, fell from the pins and cascaded along her shoulders and down to her waist like a red waterfall.

"Are you okay?" Jonah asked.

"I took a bath," Clara said, placing the plates on the table. "My feet are slippery."

The muscles in his throat tensed with a hard swallow. "This is the first time I've seen a Mennonite or Amish woman with her hair down. You … uh. Well, I understand one of the qualities that Abram must've admired about you."

Saying nothing, Clara hurried to her bedroom, her feet thumping the floor. With the door shut, she snatched a pillow from the bed and covered her face to muffle her sobs. Yes, Abram had loved her hair: loved brushing it for her, loved burying his face into it, loved telling her how it smelled like fresh air after a day of work.

"Clara?" Jonah knocked softly. "I hear crying,

are you okay? Did you hurt yourself when you slipped?"

She wiped her face and eyes with the pillowcase. She hated to lie, but she also hated to tell Jonah how much she missed Abram. "I twisted my ankle."

"Do you need a doctor?"

"It's not broken. I can put my weight on it."

"I see you have an icebox. Would you like me to wrap some ice in a towel for it? It'll help keep the swelling down."

"Please, no. Go ahead and eat. I'll be there soon."

Silence. More silence. "I hate cold pizza." Jonah's voice was soft, sincere. "Bow your head while I say the blessing."

Clara tilted her head to one side. "What?"

"I said bow—"

"I heard. You just surprised me."

A soft chuckle came from beyond the door. "I surprised you because you think a man living in sin wouldn't want to say a blessing, right?"

"I didn't mean—"

"Or a man who drinks alcohol."

"I didn't say—"

"Regardless, bow your head."

Clara did so before Jonah managed to read her thoughts—and worse, her judgements of him— again.

"Is your head bowed?"

"It is, go ahead."

"Dear Heavenly Father, thank you for the friendship I've found with my neighbor. Please comfort her and give her peace in her time of mourning. Help me understand her and her Ordnung's ways." Jonah paused. "If there's anything I can do to help her around the farm so she can provide for herself and her children, please allow me to do so. And Father, please bless the food we are about the eat. May it nourish our bodies for Your service, amen."

Jonah's footsteps thudded away from Clara's door, and she lay stunned on the bed. His blessing, mostly a prayer, was exactly what she needed to hear. Not only was it touching with its sincerity, it was beautiful with its simple message of comfort.

She rose and pinned her hair, donned her white kapp and found him in the kitchen, a slice of pizza in his hand and a glass of water by his plate. "Hey," he said, chewing with his mouth full. "You aren't limping, it's a miracle." He took a slice of pizza from the box and slid the cheesy triangle onto a plate for her. "Lemonade would've been good, but I didn't want to ramble in your icebox."

"I don't have any more made at the moment." Clara ran herself a glass of water from the sink and sat. "Would you believe I've never eaten pizza?"

Chewing again, Jonah held up a finger, but his widened eyes told her he was surprised. After his swallow, he wiped his lips with a napkin from the holder on the table. "Never eaten pizza? Eating pizza should be one of the Ten Commandments, shouldn't it?"

Clara picked up the warm slice of pizza. "I'll let you know after I try it." She bit, but the crust didn't break cleanly."

"Pull it," Jonah said. "Half the fun of pizza is seeing how long you can make the cheese stretch."

She did as he suggested, resulting in a long string of cheese that finally broke and fell into the plate. The cheese seemed to grow as she chewed, unlike the cheese she made, but the browned slices of meat were a bit spicy, like her mother's homemade sausage.

Jonah stopped chewing. "You've got grease on your chin."

Clara wiped her chin. "You said Lydia is visiting relatives in Ohio?"

"Yes."

"Don't I get to know more than that?"

"You wouldn't believe me if I told you." Jonah took another bite of pizza, as if he didn't care to go on.

Clara did the same, enjoying a piece of earthy

tasting mushroom this time.

Jonah drank water. "Do you need bedding plants or seeds for the garden? I can take you to South Boston for them, or you can make a list and I can get them for you. Do you use fertilizer? I could get that too."

"Abram plowed plenty of aged chicken manure into the soil on the day he ..." At the thought of her loving husband's death on the same day as applied the manure to the garden, Clara's hands trembled, and she dropped the pizza to the plate. She wanted to run to her bed again, wanted to do anything but wear her emotions on her sleeve in front of Jonah, who was practically a stranger.

He took a napkin from the holder, left it beside her plate, and went to the door. "I'll give you some privacy."

As the door creaked open, Clara turned toward him. "Please ... please sit. I just ... well, so many memories of Abram ... I mean ..."

Jonah returned to the table. "I would feel the same way if it were me. Love is an amazing thing when you find the right person." He gently covered both her hands with his large one. "Tell me what will help. I'll do whatever I can."

Shame flooded Clara. What she wanted was to be held and comforted, but she didn't dare ask it.

Jonah took the napkin from her still trembling

hands and wiped her cheeks. "I do this for Lydia when—" With a slight smile, he rubbed Clara's nose with the napkin. "How's that?"

Clara took the napkin. What was he hiding about Lydia? He had refused to say more about her trip to Ohio, and now he had stopped midsentence when he was about to say why he would wipe her eyes like he had wiped Clara's. "I'm sorry," she said, picking up the pizza again. "I suppose I need to learn to live without Abram eventually."

Silence filled the moment. Jonah ate. Clara ate. Both drank water. Through the screen door, the bluebird pair warbled their song. Jonah placed another slice on his plate. "Can I ask you something?"

Clara had no idea what he wanted to ask. His head tilted to one side, and his eyes focused on hers. "What is it?" she asked.

"I don't want to upset you."

"It's all right, what is it?"

"Do you think you'll ever—"

Gravel crunched in the driveway, drowning the bluebird's song. A vehicle door shut. Footsteps came up the steps and across the porch. "Mrs. Engelman, it's Bishop Silverman."

Jonah went to the door. "Hey, Vernon. You're just in time for pizza."

Bishop Silverman came in and hung his hat on the peg by the door. "Hello, Jonah. I see you've plowed the garden. That's very nice of you."

"No nicer than you allowing me to help Clara."

The bishop's eyes cut toward Clara. Apparently, he didn't care for Jonah using her first name. "Clara, yes. She has a fine name, doesn't she?"

"Yes, sir. It's a lovely name."

Clara got another plate and a glass of water and sat. "Please have some pizza."

"Don't mind if I do." Bishop Silverman placed a slice on his plate. "I never told you and Abram my first name, Clara. Then again, our small community isn't able to have church as often as we would like."

"That's right," Jonah said. "You told me it hasn't been that long since you formed your group near Nathalie. What, four years?"

"That's correct. One couple is older, and he has health issues. There's Alison and Samuel and another couple. We help each other as much as possible, but last year's crops didn't do well."

Clara noted how the bishop had used her first name. "I didn't realize you two knew each other so well."

About to take a bite of pizza, Jonah stopped. "We met in the home improvement store in South Boston a while back."

"And glad of it too," the bishop said. "I needed

a new light switch for the kitchen and wasn't sure how to install it. Jonah saw me scratching my head at the display and asked if I needed help. When I told him what I needed, he offered to install it free of charge." The bishop drank water. "I'm glad. If I had installed it myself, I might've burned my house down."

Jonah grinned. "Don't talk like that. You might scare Clara away from letting me wire her house for electricity."

"That's right," the bishop said. "You mentioned that about her when I saw you last."

At the bishop's *her*, Clara chewed her lower lip. These two were talking about *her* like she wasn't there. "Did he give you a good deal on the work?" she asked. "He looks like a crook to me."

Vernon's narrowed eyes questioned her. "Didn't you hear me say he did it for free?"

"She's got pizza in her ears," Jonah said. "I think she likes it."

"I liked it better warm," Clara said, raising another slice to her mouth.

"How's your sister?" the bishop asked Jonah.

Clara quickly swallowed the bite of pizza. "I didn't know you have a sister."

"How could you not know that when they live together?" the bishop asked.

Jonah's eyes darted from the bishop to Clara. "She's doing okay," he told the bishop.

Clara couldn't believe the interaction. It seemed Jonah was lying to the bishop about Lydia being his fiancé. Living with a woman out of wedlock, drinking alcohol, and now lying: Jonah Ellis had lowered considerably on the doorstep of her approval.

The bishop finished his slice of pizza, followed it with water, and stood. "Be right back." He left and returned with a plastic shopping bag. He placed it on the table and began taking out seed packets. "Squash, cucumbers, sweet peppers, corn. I have some seed potatoes and tomato slips in my pickup. Do you need anything else for your garden?"

"That's very nice of you," Clara said, surprised that the bishop would go to this trouble.

"How about butterbeans?" Jonah asked. "Add those to tomatoes, potatoes, corn, beef, chicken and—"

"Onions," the bishop said. "I have some of those too." He took more packets from the bag. "And here are the butterbeans. I'll set the slips on the porch, Clara. Will you and Jonah plant everything today? You've still got a few hours of sunlight left."

"I'm game if she is," Jonah said. He took another bite of pizza, chewed and swallowed. "I didn't tell you. Clara's gonna give me Bible lessons."

The bishop returned the seeds to the bag. "You told me. I guess you forgot. I'll put these on the porch too."

When the door closed, Clara faced Jonah. "I can plant my own garden, thank you very much."

"Suit yourself. If you ask your bishop, I bet he'll help. I think he'd like to ask you out on a date."

"We don't date like you English date," Clara whispered, afraid the bishop would hear through the screen door. His truck door clicked open and closed. Maybe he forgot something.

Jonah leaned close to Clara. "Your cheeks are red. I bet he'll like that. Do you want me to leave so he can help with the garden?"

Clara wanted them *both* to leave, but she wanted to ask Jonah why Bishop Silverman thought Lydia was Jonah's sister, including Jonah's remark that she wouldn't believe him if he told her about Lydia visiting her relatives. "I'd rather you stay," she said. "That's the least you can do after lying about Lyd—"

The bishop stuck his head in the door. "I left some cabbage slips also. You know how I love cabbage soup. See you soon."

As his tires crunched gravel in the driveway, Jonah tapped her hand. "Ah, you've had the good bishop over for supper and have fed him cabbage soup." He tapped her hand again. "And here I was, thinking you preferred me as a husband instead of him."

Clara stood. "You are so …" She could've said any number of discourteous things, but it wasn't the Christian thing to do.

"Infuriating?" Jonah asked through a grin. "Or maybe frustrating? What about—"

"All of the above. Finish your pizza. It'll be dark in a little while, and I want to get the garden planted."

Chapter 4

With the back of her hand, Clara wiped sweat from her forehead before it ran into her eyes. It officially turned summer yesterday, and the June sun beamed down on her, Edna, and John, all on their hands and knees as they pulled weeds from the growing garden.

John rubbed his nose, adding another smudge of dirt to the three already there. "I'm thirsty, Mama."

Edna faced Clara, her hand at the base of a tomato plant. "Doesn't Papa have a plow for weeds?" Dark soil covered her blue dress at the knees. A droplet of sweat clung to the tip of her nose. Her auburn hair, a mix of Clara and Abram's colors, hung in damp tendrils to her shoulders. Not long before Abram died, he mentioned how Edna needed to start wearing a white kapp soon, but the idea made Clara feel as if her daughter was growing up too quickly.

"I thought he did have a plow for weeds," Clara said, peering up at the bright orb of the sun in the sky, so mid-day white it glowed with blinding brilliance. Unfortunately, Jonah hadn't taught her how to drive the tractor yet. Then again, the last time he stopped by, when he plowed the garden, she had lost her patience with him and wasn't sure if she wanted him to visit again. The same went for Bishop Silverman. Both men were nice to help her, but when they had been here, her patience had run as thin as the cloth on the knees of John's pants.

A crow cawed, followed by another. Clara shaded her eyes in time to see a flock winging toward the garden, but they soon veered away. Something else to do: make one or more scarecrows to keep those feathered fiends from setting their sights on her family's food supply. The crows continued over the hill toward Jonah's farm. Clara returned to the weeds, and a shotgun blast sounded. She couldn't see the crow go down, but she had heard Jonah shooting at them before. He must think highly of his garden if he were willing to kill to protect it. Crows weren't edible, so why not make a scarecrow?

A stream of sweat trickled from one underarm and left a cool trail down her side. She had been eating less to conserve the canned food and had lost weight, which made enough room between the fabric of her blue dress and her side to allow sweat to trickle. A cool bath would be wonderful. Better yet, a cool bath with the tub filled by someone other than herself. She enjoyed the independence of hard work, but her palms had blistered and healed so much since Abram had died, her hands appeared burned. He used to love holding her hands, saying he loved how delicate they were, saying how he did much of the harder farm work to spare her hands from abuse.

Clara moved to the next tomato plant. Cringing at a cramp in the pit of her abdomen, she jerked at a huge clump of crabgrass in the middle of the row. Yes, Abram had a special plow called a cultivator for removing weeds like these. They would then use hoes to chop the weeds near the plants. If she could connect the cultivator to the tractor and drive it, not only would it save work, it would save wear and tear on her family's clothes and her from a sore back and knees from when she knelt on hidden rocks. Realization made her look toward the barn. Abram kept a fuel tank behind it. He had filled it a week before his accident, so she should have enough for the garden if she knew how to drive the tractor.

Another cramp struck, possibly from a coming

monthly cycle. Did she have one last month? She thought so, but it hid from her memory, shadowed by the grief of losing Abram.

John got up, even more dirty kneed, and tugged her arm. "Mama, when can we stop? I'm—"

An ear-shattering scream came from Edna. Slapping at her arm, she kicked away from the tomato plant she had been weeding. "Mama! A black spider bit me!"

In the dirt by the tomato plant, the crushed remains of a Black Widow spider lay, it's six legs twitching. Clara's only thought was to get Edna to the hospital in South Boston … but how?

Jonah!

She scooped Edna into her arms, told John to come with her, and ran as fast as she could toward the hill between her and Jonah's farms. *God help us,* she prayed. *Please let us get to the hospital in time. I can't lose any more of my family.*

Trailing behind her, John fell to the grass and started crying. Clara glanced back. "Do the best you can, John! I can't stop!"

Wiping his eyes, her son stopped crying and got up to run after her again.

Thank you, Lord, for making him strong like my Abram!

"It hurts," Edna whined. "Am I going to die and see Papa?"

Clara couldn't speak for her exploding breaths. Her pulse roared in her ears, sounding like thunder after multiple lightning strikes. The grass, up to her waist, snagged her shoes. Grasshoppers whirred and clattered before her as if they were leading the way. She started down the hill. Standing by the garden, Jonah set the shotgun down and ran toward her. "Clara! What—"

Ignoring his words, she burst toward him through the last fifty yards of tall grass, tripping at the last. He caught her as she fell, and Clara looked up into his eyes. "Black—" She gulped a huge breath. "Black Widow."

Panting hard, John arrived at Clara's side. "A spider bit Edna."

Jonah grabbed him up. "Get her in the pickup, Clara." He put John in the back seat. "I'll get my keys and tell Lydia."

Still breathless, Clara put Edna down, got in the truck, and took her into her arms. Jonah ran out of the house. In the truck, he gave Clara a cloth wrapped around something hard. "This has ice in it. Keep it against the bite."

As Clara pressed the cloth to the bite, Jonah backed the truck around until it faced the road. The engine roared. Gravel clattered beneath the fenders. The back tires screeched against the pavement. At each curve, the truck slung Clara to the left or to the right. Jonah gripped the steering wheel hard enough to make his knuckles white. His lips moved in what must be a continuous prayer for Edna's safety.

He glanced at Clara. "We'll be on the main road in a few minutes and at the hospital emergency room soon. They may have to give her antivenom intravenously."

Clara had never heard those words. "What does that mean?"

"Antivenom counteracts the spider's poison. A nurse will insert a hollow needle into a vein. The vein is attached to a tube. The tube runs to a bag of solution. They'll put the antivenom in the solution and it'll go into the vein."

John stuck his head between the two seats. "Will it hurt?"

Edna looked up at Clara. "Will it hurt, Mama?"

Clara didn't want to scare Edna, but a needle into a vein sounded like it would hurt.

"Only for a second," Jonah said. "You're a big girl. You can handle it."

The highway's white lines passed to the point of blurring together. Mile after mile, Clara clutched Edna to her chest. Mile after mile, John held his sister's hand. Mile after mile, Clara and Jonah prayed.

At the emergency room entrance, he hopped out and opened Clara's door. The foursome hurried inside, and Jonah went to the receptionist's window. "We need help for a Black Widow bite."

Shoving a pad and pen toward Jonah, the receptionist asked for Edna's name. Jonah shoved it back. "Ma'am, you can get that information later. You either get someone out here now, or I'll take her back myself."

The woman's eyes darted between Jonah and Clara. "Spider bites are rarely fatal."

Jonah placed his hand in the small of Clara's back and led her to a set of double doors to the left. Inside the area, a nurse showed her palm. "Sir, you can't come back here."

Jonah's jaw muscles tightened. "This little girl was bitten by a Black Widow about twenty minutes ago. You can help her now, or I start tearing this place apart."

The receptionist burst through the doors and told the nurse that security was on the way. To the right, a door opened to reveal a young man with a name tag that said he was a doctor. "I heard that," he said. "Take her to the next treatment area. I just finished my patient."

Clara silently thanked God—not only for Jonah but for this doctor. In the treatment area, she lay

Edna on a bed and removed the dripping cloth wrapped around the melting ice. The bite, swollen and red, looked much worse than earlier.

The doctor gently touched it, and Edna jerked her arm away. Concern tightened his lips into a thin line. "Does it hurt, sweetheart?" Edna nodded. He leaned closer to Edna's face, then faced Clara. "Her eyes look swollen to me. Do they to you?"

"Maybe a little," Clara said, wondering why that was important.

"What about her lips?" he asked.

"Yes, a little."

Edna grabbed her throat and wheezed. The doctor ran out and returned with a nurse, who held a bag a liquid.

"What's wrong?" Clara asked. "Will she be all right?"

The doctor opened a pouch of some kind, releasing something that smelled of alcohol, and wiped the inside of Edna's arm above her elbow. "She's going into anaphylaxis. We've got to administer antivenom."

The doctor held Edna's arm. The nurse inserted a needle and Edna screamed. "You're hurting her!" Clara yelled.

The doctor faced Jonah. "Sir, please get your wife out of here."

Jonah took Clara by the arm. "They're doing the

right thing, Clara. I told you this might happen." He led her and John to a waiting room not far from the receptionist area. Edna's scream still rang in Clara's ears. She sat and rocked back and forth. John sat beside her and held her hand. Jonah brought them drinks from a machine and opened them. John took his. Clara refused hers.

Time passed with prayer after prayer. Clara begged and pleaded, but dread filled her—the same dread as the day Abram had fallen from the hay loft. She finally sipped the drink, sweet and fizzy. She'd rather have water.

John threw his can away. Jonah slowly sipped his. The doors to the treatment area opened. Clara whirled toward them, but she didn't recognize the person. By the clock on the wall, this happened twice in the next hour.

A mother came in with her son. He had fallen off his bike and broken his arm. She filled out paperwork. They were taken back ten minutes later. Clara stood. Without insurance, she would have to set up payments. As she started toward the receptionist to tell her, a deep pain in her lower stomach doubled her over. Something warm and wet ran down her leg. The next thing she knew, Jonah was catching her as she lost consciousness.

Chapter 5

Someone's voice drew Clara back to consciousness, but she was too tired to open her eyes. Like a morning fog in the field at the foot of the hill between her and Jonah's homes, weariness covered her from head to toe. She must be in bed at home. Morning sun filled the room, bright enough to see through closed eyelids. Abram must be letting her rest from the previous day's chores. Footsteps came closer. She smelled some kind of food. A hand touched hers. "Mrs. Engelman?"

Clara rolled over to cry. She must be dreaming about Bishop Silverman speaking to her after Abram died.

A hand touched her shoulder. "I know you're upset about Edna, but you need to eat."

Edna?

Clara bolted upright. She wore a thin gown of

some kind. Her hair flowed down her shoulders. A bandage covered the end of a tube that ran from her arm to a bag of liquid like the one the doctor had used for Edna in the emergency room. The bag hung from a metal stand. Beside her in a chair, Bishop Silverman patted her hand. "Welcome back to the land of the living. You've been unconscious for almost twenty-four hours."

She shoved his hand away. "Where's Edna? Why am I in this bed? Is she all right? Where's John?" Another question faltered within her weary mind, one that surprised her with its urgency.

Where's Jonah?

"John's with Jonah and his sister. Edna's in intensive care. She had a reaction from the antivenom." The bishop paused. "I hate to tell you this, but she's on a ventilator."

"I … I don't know what that is."

"It helps a person breathe until they can breathe on their own."

A nurse came in. "Sir, I need to check Mrs. Engelman's vital signs."

Bishop Silverman stood. "I'll be right back."

The nurse studied the screen of a machine with a rising and falling line and noted something on a pad. "Please," Clara said. "Can I see my daughter?"

"After you've eaten," she said, nodding toward

a tray of food on a stand to the side of the bed. "You lost a lot of blood during your miscarriage, and you need to build your strength up."

Clara fell back to the pillow. She hadn't even known she was expecting, much less that she had missed her last monthly cycle. It must've happened from not eating regularly, along with overwork. The urge to weep overwhelmed her. She had lost Abram's child—another child of his to love.

On the windowsill to her left, a vase of daisies caught her eye. Bishop Silverman must've brought them, a sincere gesture of caring.

The nurse jotted another note. "I'll see you later. Please try to eat."

Bishop Silverman entered as she left. Embarrassed at not being dressed, Clara pulled the sheet to her chin. "I know why I'm here." Heat filled her cheeks. She didn't care to talk about her womanly issues with a man who wasn't Abram.

The bishop rolled the stand with the tray of food over. "Let's try this meatloaf." He forked a bite, sniffed it and frowned. "I'm sure it's not as good as your own."

Clara preferred to eat her own cooking, but she wanted to see Edna. She took the fork. Bringing it to her mouth, she dropped it on the sheet. "Where's John?"

Drinking soda from a can, the bishop lowered it.

"I told you, John's with Jonah and his sister. You really need to eat if you forgot already."

Clara didn't know if Lydia was Jonah's sister or his fiancé. Hadn't he told her they were engaged? Regardless, it was none of her business. He was nothing to her but a decent neighbor who had helped her from time to time … and who had saved Edna's life by bringing her here … and who had plowed the garden … and who had helped sow the seeds … and now, who had welcomed John into his home.

A man who did those things might be interested in her for another reason. Since he was engaged, he and Lydia were simply being neighborly—nothing more, nothing less. Bishop Silverman, however, had brought flowers and was willing to feed her. Although she had shied away from him back in April—both because he had almost touched her hair and from the rumor that his wife had left him—he was here now, unlike Jonah.

Wiping her eyes still wet from crying, Clara heaved a sigh. She took a napkin from the tray and wiped the meatloaf from the sheet. The bishop laughed. "I drop my food too, and I don't have the reason you have. I'm sorry for your loss. I'm sure it's much harder because Abram is gone."

"It is." Clara forked more meatloaf. "I miss him

more than I can say."

The bishop swallowed more soda. "In case you were wondering, Jonah told me what happened with Edna. I'm glad he was there for you. He's very helpful."

Clara ate mashed potatoes. The bishop drank soda. "You know how small our community is," he said. "It's a shame we can't persuade Jonah and his sister to join us."

The question confused Clara. It took more than someone being helpful to join the Amish, including the Beachy Amish Mennonites. It took a sincere desire to follow their Ordnung. It also took the desire to not lie, like Jonah and Lydia may be doing about their engagement. And to think, John was with them at this very moment.

Done with the meal, Clara pushed the stand away. "If I have to stay here another night, I'd rather Alison could keep John."

"I told her that," the bishop said. "One of her children has a bad cold. He's in good hands with Jonah."

"But he's English," Clara blurted.

The bishop tilted his head to one side. "We're all God's children. 'Judge not lest ye be judged.'"

Clara ignored the remark. As a parent, her children were her responsibility and no one else's, especially not an English person's responsibility.

She and Edna would get well and go home. The last place in the world she wanted to be was in the house of a pair of sinners like Jonah and Lydia, his so-called sister.

Bishop Silverman stood. "I should be going. Jonah said to tell you he found your keys in the kitchen and has locked the house. He fed the chickens and gathered the eggs too. They're in a basket in the kitchen. I was going to milk the cow so she wouldn't go dry, but he did it."

"Why would the cow go dry?" Clara asked. "That takes longer than a day."

"He's making sure. Like I told you, Edna's on a ventilator. It might be a while before she can come home, and you'll want to stay here." The bishop took cash from his wallet and left it on the nightstand. "Consider this a gift for food after you're discharged." He took his wide-brimmed hat from a table in the corner. "I'll see you soon."

Minutes later, someone knocked on the door. A middle-aged woman with reading glasses perched on the end of her nose peeked in. "I'm Mrs. Talbot, from the billing department."

With her heart sinking, Clara told the woman to come in. "I need to set up payments. That's all I can afford."

Smiling, the woman sat in the chair by the bed

that the bishop had just left. "Although we don't know the total yet, someone made a credit card payment on it."

Blinking with curiosity, Clara wondered who would do such a thing. Maybe Bishop Silverman had called her parents in Pennsylvania, and they made the payment. "Did the person leave a name?"

"He did."

"Can you tell me?"

"I'm afraid not. We take the privacy of clients very seriously here." Mrs. Talbot leaned toward Clara. "I can tell you this—he said he set up a GoFundMe account to help."

Clara narrowed her eyes. "A what?"

Mrs. Talbot straightened. "It's on the internet. A person makes a profile that says why they need money. People then donate if they'd like." She stood. "He said your bill is covered so far. Being Mennonite, isn't it nice to know someone cares about you so much along with God?" She went to the door. "Your bishop gave us your address. We'll send any unpaid bills there."

The nurse came in. "I see you finished your lunch. Let's get a robe on you so I can roll your IV down the hall. Then you can see your daughter."

Despite feeling naked, Clara allowed the nurse to wheel her along in a wheelchair, pushing the IV stand at the same time. Most of the young men who passed glanced at her, no doubt attracted to her half-clothed state and her flowing red hair. The nurse stopped at a room filled with chairs. In one, Jonah stood and came over to kiss Clara's cheek. "Hey, sweetheart. Edna's doctor said you would be along after you ate." He lingered near Clara's ear. "I sure miss you at home." He moved closer. "I told them I was your husband yesterday," he whispered, "so play along."

Clara didn't care for Jonah's kiss one bit, but she would allow it since he had saved Edna's life. "Fine, let's see our daughter. I've been worried to death about her."

The nurse took them to the intensive care unit. A row of beds lined a wall. Curtains separated each patient from the next. Some were unconscious, some not. Tubes and wires ran to various monitors. When she stopped the chair beside Edna, Clara burst into tears.

A tube entered her small mouth, tape holding it in place. The other end connected to a machine. Each time the tube pulsed, Edna's small chest rose and fell as if she were part of the machine.

Clara couldn't help herself. Crying terribly, she reached for Jonah, who leaned over to wrap his arms around her. "Shh, sweetheart, she's going to be okay. We have to have faith, right?" The next thing Clara knew, Jonah was sobbing and she was holding him as tightly as he was holding her. She didn't know how long they held each other, how long they cried together, but it felt wonderful to be held by a man whose arms were so much like Abram's: strong and firm, loving and kind. Done with her cry, she pulled away to kiss Jonah's cheek. "You're right, sweetheart. We have to remember to have faith."

A sudden question spun from Clara's mind. Was she falling in love with Jonah, not only an English man but an engaged man?

No!

She loved Abram and no one else. No other man would ever take his place. Yes, she may eventually marry. To not would deny Edna and John a father in the home to complete their family, something the Beachy Amish—and all Amish—valued.

The nurse rolled the wheelchair closer. "I'll let you three alone for a moment. You can't stay long, Mrs. Engelman. You need your rest too."

Clara was afraid to touch Edna's hand, afraid she would break like Abram had broken when he fell from the hay loft. She faced Jonah. His eyes were still red from crying. "How's John?"

"He's fine. Lydia's taking good care of him."

Bishop Silverman said you were doing things around the house. Thank you for that, and thank you for saving Edna's life."

Jonah shared a hesitant smile. "Of course I'd save her, sweetheart. That's what dads do when they love their families." His cheeks reddened. 'Well, you know what I mean. That's what good neighbors—and people—do."

Silence fell between them as they watched Edna. Jonah smoothed a lock of hair at her temple. "You stay strong, Edna. We all need you back in the neighborhood." He faced Clara. "Your doctor told me about the baby." He looked away and back, as if something was on his mind. "When Edna can leave the hospital, both of you need help until you get well again. I want y'all to stay with Lydia and me. I've already mentioned it, and she agrees."

The suggestion both surprised and appalled Clara. She wanted to discover if Lydia and Jonah were engaged, or if they were brother and sister— only to know the truth of course, not because she was attracted to him—but to stay with them with that goal in mind felt dishonest, even like she planned to spy on them.

Shaking her head, she told Jonah she couldn't accept any more of his hospitality, to which he snorted derisively. "Hospitality my eye. My home is your home, and that's the end of it."

On the sheet beside Edna, her hand trembled.

Then her fingers opened and closed, opened and closed, and her eyes fluttered open. Jonah got a nurse from next door, and Clara lowered her head to thank God for yet another miracle in her life.

Chapter 6

Six days later, Jonah opened the pickup door for Clara, who eased Edna to her feet. Clara climbed out behind her, followed by John. A summer rain, soft and warm, was falling. Jonah picked up Edna and faced Clara. "I got her. Let's hurry before we get wet."

On the front porch of the huge farmhouse, Lydia opened the door. Cut short and stylish, dark hair framed her face. Like Jonah, she wore blue jeans and tennis shoes. She, however, wore a yellow blouse instead of a plain red T-shirt like Jonah wore. Although her brown eyes focused on Clara, Clara couldn't ignore Lydia's left arm. It bent at an angle at her elbow, almost if it were a chicken's broken wing.

She quickly looked into Lydia's questioning stare, afraid she had caught her. "Thank you so much for allowing us into your home."

Lydia waved the comment away. "Like Jonah said, we wouldn't be good neighbors if we didn't help."

Inside the large living room, Jonah set Edna down. She still had a bandage on her arm where the spider had bitten her. John came over, and they obediently went to a sofa and sat. Clara admired the room. At each end of the sofa, two easy chairs waited for someone to relax. At the far side of the room, a huge fireplace beckoned, though nothing burned in it at the moment. In a corner to the left of the fireplace, a desk sat with a short stack of papers on it.

"Sorry about the mess," Jonah said. "I've been making plans to finish your electrical system."

"You've done too much already," Clara said.

Lydia crossed the room and pushed a button. Behind Clara, cool air blew from a grate next to the wall. "I love air conditioning," Lydia said. "You will too when you have it."

Clara started to say she couldn't afford it, but shame stopped her. Ever since the woman at the hospital told her how someone had paid her bill, she wondered who the person was. Jonah and Bishop Silverman never failed to mention helping Clara whenever they did, so it couldn't be them. She had also asked her father about the bill when she had called to tell him and her mother about Edna's spider bite, and he had said no, to count it as a gift from God, because if the person who did it wanted to remain anonymous, it truly *was* a gift from God. Mama had offered to come help Clara until she felt better, but Clara didn't want to put her out.

Lydia joined Clara. "Our home is your home. Can Jonah take you home for some clothes for you and the children?"

"Bring my toys," John said.

"And my dolls," Edna said. She yawned. "I'm tired."

Lydia sat beside her. "If your mother doesn't mind, we can take your kapp off so you can rest on the sofa."

John hopped up and gave Jonah his wide-brimmed straw hat. Grinning, Jonah hung it on a rack by the door. "Let's get your things, Clara."

When Jonah parked in Clara's driveway, she couldn't believe her eyes. No weeds choked the garden. Green tomatoes shined, wet with rain, and yellow squash too. The corn was half grown. Green beans were filling out. She faced Jonah. "I don't know how to thank you for keeping the weeds down. I think the spider bit Edna because it could hide in them."

Jonah pointed toward the barn. "You ran out of chicken feed, so I bought a new bag. You can add the price to the total for when I complete your electrical work. Right now you can thank me by getting out of the rain."

On the porch, he unlocked the door and opened it for Clara. The table held one small basket of eggs. Puzzled, Clara picked one up. "I thought there would be more eggs than this."

Jonah neared her. "I hope you don't mind, but I sold the rest at the market." From his wallet, he gave her two twenty- dollar bills, two tens, one five, and three ones.

Clara started to put the money in a dress pocket. Instead, she offered it to Jonah. "Let me pay you for the chicken feed and your work on the garden. Gas is expensive."

Jonah picked up an egg. "Maybe you can make me breakfast sometime. I love a soft-boiled egg. He put the egg back. "Besides, selling the eggs was Bishop Silverman's idea."

Clara put the money in her pocket. It seemed Bishop Silverman was almost as nice as Jonah.

Jonah opened the icebox. "Here's some tomatoes I picked this morning. Your green beans are coming along nicely. They'll be ready to can soon."

Clara didn't answer. She needed to get over the miscarriage and bring her family home and get to work. First, she needed some clothes for everyone.

As she turned to leave for her bedroom, pain hit in her lower stomach, nearly doubling her over. Her doctor said this might happen. Jonah offered a hand, and she took it until the pain faded. Again, like when Jonah had comforted her in the hospital, his brown eyes were kind and concerned. The pain eased. She drew herself up, hardly to his shoulder. The woman in her wanted to press her face to his chest and have him hold her. The Beachy Amish woman in her screamed that she was sinning to even think such a thing, screamed to ignore her feelings, screamed to set aside all thoughts of herself as if she were a— In her mind, those thoughts faltered. She wasn't an unfeeling robot. She was a strong and vital woman who God had blessed in more ways than she could count.

Jonah's kind eyes searched hers. "I know you miss Abram, Clara. You've been through so much in hardly no time at all. I wish …"

The question of his relationship with Lydia aggravated Clara. If they weren't engaged, he could join the Beachy Amish Mennonites and they could get—

She went to the table and pretended to count eggs. How could she think they could get married? She was a sinful woman, thinking with the flesh instead of with God's word, as well as ignoring the memory of Abram. Without facing Jonah, she cleared her throat. "These are some nice eggs. We can take some to your house."

She hesitated. Why couldn't Jonah turn her around and share his feelings? He must have them, or he wouldn't be helping her so much.

Jonah eased her around by her shoulders. "I was going to say I wish you could find someone to love as much as you loved Abram. I realize it's too soon, but you can find someone eventually. Don't take this the wrong way, but what do you think of Bishop Silverman? He seems like a nice guy."

Jonah's words shriveled Clara's heart. No matter how ashamed she was of her feelings for him, she couldn't deny them, and all he wanted was for her to offer herself to someone else. Steeling herself for a desperate question, she faced him. "You once said you and Lydia were engaged. Then Bishop Silverman said you were brother and sister. Which is it?"

Jonah crossed his arms. "You should get your clothes so we can go."

"Why won't you tell me?"

"Why is it important?"

Clara looked away and back. "Because truth is important. Anything other than the truth is a lie."

Heaving a huge sigh, Jonah ran his fingers

through his hair. "You want to know the truth? The truth is I'm attracted to you. I pray and pray and pray and pray for the strength to overcome my feelings, but I can't."

His admission, the one she had been wanting to hear, stunned Clara. She dropped to a chair before she fell. "I know it's wrong—more wrong than anything I've ever done—but I'm attracted to you too. I shouldn't have asked about Lydia. What she is to you is none of my business."

Jonah licked his lips. "Regardless of our feelings, I still want to be friends. You and your children need help, and Lydia and I are willing to do the Christian thing."

Clara stood. "I … I'll get my things." In her room, she closed the door and fell to her bed, sobbing with shame. How could she have feelings for Jonah? If Abram could look down from Heaven and see her, he would regret the day they met. Even Jonah—*English* Jonah—had said he and Lydia were willing to do the Christian thing, while she herself had been willing to throw herself at him as if she were a harlot in the Bible.

Yes, one day she would get married, but she wouldn't marry for love. Love was a once in a lifetime commitment, like what she had with her sweet Abram. What she felt for Jonah was desire—

and desire only. Yes, like Abram, he was kind and gentle. Unlike Abram, he was meant for someone else, possibly Lydia, possibly not. Regardless, his choice didn't concern Clara. She would accept his and Lydia's help for her children's sake, and for their sake alone.

At her dresser mirror, she palmed the tears from her eyes hard enough to feel her cheekbones. It was time to be a proper Beachy Amish Mennonite woman and settle this thing with Jonah once and for all.

In the kitchen again, she went to the table and sat across from him, where he was rolling an egg from one palm to the other. "I apologize for what happened," she said. "I'm … I haven't been myself since I lost Abram. We were very close, and I miss that closeness." She fluttered a hand in the air. "I'm just a silly woman who can't do anything around here. I don't like depending on anyone. Although I appreciate how the Beachy Amish help each other, I'd rather learn things so I can help myself. Does that make sense?"

"I like independent women." Jonah kept rolling the egg. "I meant what I said about finishing the wiring in your house. I'm willing to teach you to drive your tractor and your truck too. Then you can be the independent woman you want to be."

Clara touched his hand. "Can we forget what

happened? If it will help, I can still teach you about the Bible."

To her relief, Jonah laughed. "We can consider it payback for my work around here. If I waited for your chickens to lay enough eggs to pay to wire your house, I'd be an old man." He returned the egg to the basket. "What *do* you think of Bishop Silverman? You know, as a future husband? Like a far, far, far in the future husband?"

Clara had to laugh as well. Jonah's face was screwed up into the cutest expression, both boyish and handsome at the same time. She had never thought of the bishop romantically, but like she had already decided, if she married again, it wouldn't be for love. Regardless, it would be a long time before she would consider marriage again.

Jonah got up and went to the corner of the kitchen that was used as the living area. He returned with a wooden truck and a doll. Clara left to pack clothes for her and the children and returned with everything in a laundry basket. Despite the rain, the day was warm, and sweat trickled from her underarms.

Jonah wiped his brow and asked if she had everything. She said she did, so they climbed into his truck.

At his house again, Clara unpacked the clothes

on the bed Lydia had shown her. The children were asleep on the sofa. Jonah came in. "I hope this room is okay." He went to a cot he had set up for John. "At least the bed's big enough for you and Edna." His cheek's reddened. "I should go." Instead of leaving, he went to the bed and fluffed the pillow. Then he ran his fingertips across it.

Unless Clara missed her guess, he was thinking about running his fingertips through her hair.

He pulled his hand away. "I should go. You need to rest."

Clara nodded. "Where's the bathroom? I would like a bath first."

"We only have showers. You saw Lydia's arm. She would have to support herself to sit in a tub, so we remodeled the bathrooms to have only showers."

Clara wanted to ask about Lydia's arm but didn't want to pry. Nodding, she went to Jonah. He led her down a hall and stopped at the first door. "You and the children can use this bathroom." He pointed. "The next room is mine and the second one is Lydia's. The room across the hall is our bathroom." He opened the door to Clara's bathroom. She followed him in, where he gestured toward a huge shower. "I put this in myself."

Clara marveled at Jonah's work. The shower was large enough for two people. Gleaming tiles of some kind formed the walls. A single showerhead as large as a plate pointed down from the ceiling. "Why didn't you install a curtain or a door?"

Jonah turned the water on. "The showerhead is supposed to mimic rain. It doesn't splatter, so it doesn't need a door." He opened a door across from the shower. "Towels and washcloths are in here. Shampoo and soap are in the cabinet under the sink." He went to the sink, where a hair dryer hung from a hanger on the wall. "With all that hair of yours, you might want to dry it." He started to leave but stopped in the doorway. "Do you and the children like spaghetti? That's what Lydia is making for supper."

"Anything is fine," Clara said. "Please thank her for welcoming us into your home."

Jonah closed the door, and Clara leaned against the sink. So, he and Lydia slept in different rooms, which increased the mystery of their relationship. At best they were brother and sister. At worst they were engaged and were waiting for marriage before they shared a bedroom. No, at worst, the thought of Jonah's availability as a future husband was still planted firmly in Clara's mind—a thought she needed to rid herself of starting right now.

* * *

Supper came and went without incident. Clara

had enjoyed the gentle trickle of warm water in the shower. She even enjoyed the sweet floral aroma of the shampoo and the speed with which she could dry her hair. Even though Lydia's spaghetti sauce had come from a jar, she mixed cooked ground beef with it, creating a delicious meal. Clara insisted on washing the dishes, doing so now. The rain had stopped, so Jonah was outside, planning where to build a fence for his first herd of beef cattle, due in a month. John and Edna were in the living room, quietly playing with their toys. Through the window over the sink, Clara watched Jonah as he paced, noting the distances on a pad.

To her right, Lydia took a dish from the strainer. She dried it with a towel and put it in a cabinet. "You should've let me wash the dishes. Wouldn't you like to rest?"

"I got tired of sitting in that hospital. It feels good to be useful." Clara put a glass in the strainer. Jonah made more notes on the pad.

"He sure is a worker," Lydia said. "I don't know what I'd do without him."

Clara kept hoping Lydia would say something to hint at her and Jonah's relationship, but each statement was vague.

Lydia took another dish from the strainer. "Jonah said he'll teach you to drive sometime. I understand the Amish and Mennonites in communities that don't drive hire drivers to take them places. You should hire him to take you and the kids to the lake in Clarksville, or to the beach at the Outer Banks. Both are amazing. We rented a pontoon boat at the lake a few weekends ago and went fishing. I can't tell you how relaxing it was." Lydia dried the dish. "I saw two Amish ladies selling flowers in Clarksville the other day. Have you thought about selling eggs and vegetables there? Then you could get your house wired sooner and enjoy the air conditioning." She put the dish in the cabinet. "We have a tent we use for shade at the beach. You'll need that for shade. I'm sure Jonah will be glad to drive you."

Despite Lydia's generous offer, Clara wondered how her arm had been hurt. Sticking out at the elbow, it looked painful. It also had a faded scar along the inside of the joint.

"Don't worry about it," Lydia said. "It's not as painful as it looks."

"Do you mind if I ask what happened?" Clara almost cringed as she asked the question. Between telling Jonah she was attracted to him and asking Lydia about her arm, she had become a sinful woman and a curious busybody. The thought made her think of her best friend, Alison, who loved to gossip. In fact, Alison had gossiped about Bishop

Silverman, saying his wife had left him for another man, only to file for divorce a year later. Clara wondered what would cause such a thing. Every time she turned around, it seemed someone she knew was keeping secrets. Then again, she was keeping the secret of her attraction to Jonah from Lydia. Sister or not, fiancé or not, that secret probably wouldn't be revealed until either Jonah or Lydia admitted their exact relationship, or until they got married. She wore no engagement ring, and there were no intimate photographs of them around the house, so that secret might stay a secret for quite some time.

Lydia waved the question about her arm away. "Oh, it was just an accident."

The desire to ask what kind of accident could result in a surgery on an arm filled Clara with curiosity. Her visit here had yielded yet another secret. At this rate, the more she knew about Jonah and Lydia, the less she actually knew.

Jonah came in. "How's it going, ladies?"

"Almost done," Lydia said. She dried and placed the last glass in the cabinet. "I was telling Clara about going fishing on the lake. Let's all go when she and Edna feel up to it."

Behind them pattered footsteps. "Fishin'?" John asked. "Can I go?"

"Me too," Edna said, stopping beside him. "I'm

tired of doing nothing. I did that in the hospital."

Clara knelt beside them. "I need a little more time, okay? I should be able to go in another week or so."

"Good deal," Jonah said. "I'll call and reserve a pontoon boat for the weekend after next."

"I told Clara you could take her to Clarksville to sell eggs and vegetables," Lydia said. "I'll air our tent out tomorrow."

"That's a good idea," Jonah said. "A lot of people camp across from Clarksville in the summer at Occoneechee State Park. They'll love having fresh vegetables. Let me make that call about the pontoon boat."

Clara took John and Edna to the living room. Despite her attraction to Jonah, God was blessing her with friends like him and Lydia. Perhaps she wasn't turning into a sinner after all.

Chapter 7

At the end of the dock in Occoneechee State Park, where the pontoon boats were rented, Clara and the children waited while Jonah loaded a cooler filled with bottled water and sandwiches into one of the three boats. Lydia gave her a shopping bag from the local grocery store in Clarksville. "Hold our snacks while I get the rods and reels."

Clara took the bag. She didn't care for fishing, but the mile wide lake took her breath away. She and Abram had never been to Clarksville, preferring to shop either in Keysville or South Boston, so the lake was a welcome surprise.

Lydia returned with the rods and reels. Jonah, wearing shorts, a baseball cap, and a T-shirt, offered Clara his hand. "Let me help you in. You might hang your dress on the dock."

Clara took his hand, intensely aware of his touch, which she had missed since they're interaction at her house two weeks ago, when she slipped in the kitchen. She lifted the hem of her sky-blue dress and stepped into the boat. Jonah hopped onto the dock and handed John and Edna over. On a seat, Clara patted the vinyl covering for Edna and John to sit. Lydia sat beside Jonah. He inserted a key into the ignition and leaned back to cross his hands behind his head. "Ah, this is the life."

"Shouldn't we untie the boat?" Clara asked. "We can't go anywhere unless we untie the boat, right?"

Edna giggled. "You're funny, Mama."

John eyed Edna and then Clara. "Can we fish now?"

"Not yet," Lydia said, taking a bottle of water from the cooler. She opened it and gave it to Edna. "You two share this. He must be late." She took out another bottle and offered it to Clara, who refused it.

"Who else is coming?" she asked.

Jonah pointed toward the top of the dock that slanted upward toward the bank. "That's who."

Bishop Silverman waved. "I'm sorry I'm late. I had to stop in town and get my fishing license." He got in the boat, tipped his hat at Clara, and sat beside her. "I think it's time we lose the formality.

Clara, if you remember, my name is Vernon, after my father."

Lydia gave a slight shudder. "I sure wouldn't want to be named after my father."

Clara thought the comment was strange. She didn't know of any girls named after their fathers.

Jonah untied the boat and returned to the seat. "All right. Let's find some fish."

Out on the lake, after they passed several buoys that Jonah explained were there to keep people from going too fast, he pushed the throttle forward. The motor roared. The bow rose. The wind increased, folding the brim of Vernon's straw hat back. He took it off and stuck it under his leg, saying he didn't want to lose it. John's age and their Ordnung didn't require a hat yet, so Clara hadn't made him wear one today, plus Jonah had said the metal canopy would keep them from getting sunburned. Edna and her, however, wore their white kapps.

Vernon nudged Clara's arm with his. "There are times I wish I was English. Shorts like Jonah's and Lydia's would be a lot cooler."

Clara couldn't argue that. Despite the wind from the speeding boat that fluttered the hem of her dress, briefly revealing her knees, she was quite warm. The wind also loosened her hair, and red tendrils of it escaped the kapp at her temples.

To her right, a low bridge connected this side of the wide lake to the other side, where the town of Clarksville welcomed vacationers with two lakeside hotels. To the left, the rising span of a second bridge arced and curved over the lake to bypass the town. On the drive here, Lydia had recommended they return in July to walk the streets for something called "Lakefest," when vendors sold crafts and food. Jonah had added how the town held a fireworks display on the same night from the low bridge.

In the center of the lake, a boat pulled someone riding two boards strapped to their feet. Clara had never seen such a thing. She had also never seen a person half-naked in public like this one. The woman wore nothing but a bra and panties, both a bright pink. The bishop might not have seen such a thing either. He watched her until the boat pulled her beneath the low bridge and turned behind the rock fill that constructed its beginning section on this side of the lake. Jonah winked at Clara, but she didn't understand why. It seemed sinful to wear clothes that left nothing to the imagination.

Nearing the underside of the high, arcing bridge, Jonah slowed the boat and approached one of the concrete pillars. Within a few feet of it, he turned the motor off and took several life jackets from a compartment and handed them out. "I forgot about these. Keep them close while we fish, but we should wear them while we're moving." He dropped an anchor, which made a *ker-plunk* sound in the water.

Within minutes, he and Lydia had baited lines with small fish they called minnows and had cast them near the concrete pillar. Red and white floats bobbed up and down in the water. John and Edna held their rods, intent on the floats, and so did the bishop. Clara couldn't get used to the idea of calling him Vernon. It was as if Jonah had planned the day to bring her and him together, especially since his invitation had been kept a secret from her.

After several minutes without the floats going down to mark a bite, Vernon faced her. "Jonah tells me you're going to sell eggs and vegetables in Clarksville. You'll do well during the camping season."

Clara said nothing. The lake was so beautiful, shimmering in the sun. She could even smell its watery aroma. She wished Abram was with her and the children.

Edna looked up at her. "What's wrong, Mama?"

"I … something's in my eye." Clara wiped a tear from the corner of one eye. "I got it."

John jumped from the seat. "I gotta bite!" He turned to climb up on his knees and almost went over, but Jonah reached over and grabbed his belt.

"Whoa there. You're more important to us than a fish. Reel it in while I hold you."

Grunting, John reeled and reeled. "It's too big."

"Give it to me," the bishop said, reaching for the rod.

John jerked it away. "No, sir," he said firmly, similar to how Abram used to tell him the same thing when he wanted something he couldn't have.

Watching the scene, Lydia smiled. "My brother sure loves your kids, Clara."

Clara had to stop her mouth from falling open. Jonah and Lydia were brother and sister after all. At least that secret had been told. Still, her moment of hope that Jonah was available sank into the lake. He would never join her community, much less marry her. For the children's sake, the best thing she could do was to eventually settle for a decent Beachy Amish Mennonite man.

John wrestled the fish into the boat. Its scales were silver. Its mouth opened and closed, opened and closed.

"That's a nice crappie, John," Jonah said.

Edna frowned. "It looks like it's trying to kiss someone."

"All fish do that when you catch them," Lydia said.

"But why?" Edna asked.

"It's trying to breathe," the bishop said.

Edna clambered down from the vinyl seat, unhooked the fish, and threw it back in the lake. "Bye, fish! Now you can breathe!"

Clara expected John to cry. Instead, he waved too. "Bye, fish. See you later!"

Falling back to his seat, Jonah cackled laughter. "I love fried crappie, but it looks like we're catching and releasing today."

"I like fried fish too," the bishop said, disappointment in his voice. "You shouldn't have done that, Edna. The adults decide things, not you children."

Jonah and Lydia eyed each other. The bishop turned to watch his float. Clara asked for a bottle of water. Lydia gave her that and a sandwich. John and Edna asked for a sandwich and more water too. Everyone ate except the bishop, who refused to join in.

Although Clara believed their Ordnung about men ruling the household, she also believed discipline should be discussed. Abram rarely talked sharply to the children like the bishop just did, and she didn't like it. He wasn't their father, so he should defer to her.

The afternoon dragged on. The cool shade of the bridge overhead moved with the sun. Vehicle tires thumped by every few seconds. No one caught any more fish. When the children asked where the bathroom was, Jonah pulled the anchor and cranked the motor. Back at the dock, he told Clara about the bathroom near the parking area.

By the time everyone was through, Jonah and Lydia had loaded his truck with everything, and the bishop was standing with them, disappointment written in his frown. "Thank you for inviting me, Jonah. I sure wish we could've caught some fish." He faced Clara. "Regardless, I enjoyed spending the day with you, Clara." He knelt before John and Edna. "I'm sorry I snapped at you, okay?"

Edna looked up at Clara. "Papa didn't snap."

"I'm sure he didn't," the bishop said. "He was a fine husband and father. I can only hope to be the same one day." He glanced at Clara, made his goodbyes, and left for his car.

On the way home in the back seat of Jonah's truck, Clara considered the day's events. Jonah and Lydia were brother and sister. He was as kind to the children as Abram had been, not scolding them about the fish. The bishop, however, had snapped at them, but at least he had sincerely apologized for it like Abram did whenever he spoke harshly to them, as rare as that had been.

The bishop's age escaped Clara. The hair at his

temples held a hint of gray, and fine lines etched the corners of his eyes, so he was older than her at twenty-five. His interest in her was obvious, plopping down beside her on the boat and calling her Clara. Then again, on the day at her house, when he mentioned how he had never noticed her red hair, she had thought he was interested in her then as well. No one in their community had spoken ill of him. About the only negative was Alison's gossip about his wife divorcing him.

On highway 15 north, the truck bounced over the beginning of the bridge that spanned a creek that fed the lake, so Jonah had said during the drive to the park. Along the shore, boats of all kinds were tied to docks.

Bishop Silverman—Clara still couldn't think of him as Vernon no matter how hard she tried—was respected in their community north of Nathalie. He might make a decent father for the children and a good provider for her, but she doubted love would ever bloom between them, at least on her part.

Before she met Abram, her father had wanted her to marry in their community in Pennsylvania. One or two young men had caught her eye, but they were more interested in her looks than her heart. There had also been one young man named Noah she liked, but then she had met her kind and gentle Abram, and she had never looked at another man with serious interest again.

Until Jonah.

On the headrest in front of her, his brown hair beckoned her fingertips. On the console between him and Lydia, his hand begged to be held. In the rear-view mirror, his brown eyes glanced back at her, followed by a quick smile. After they had admitted their attraction for each other, how could he torture her like that, especially now that she knew he was Lydia's brother?

Shame warmed Clara's cheeks. Although she had dreamed of her wedding night with Abram before they were married, it wasn't the same as now. Now, with her experience as a fulfilled woman, her desire went beyond her girlish dreams of lying in Abram's arms on their first honeymoon night, unsure of what he expected from her. Clara was tempted to laugh. He had been as unsure as she had been, which made their becoming acquainted with each other even more— She hated to think the word, but some of the verses in the Song of Solomon in the Bible described "desire" quite clearly, such as her favorite: *Let him kiss me with the kisses of his mouth: for thy love is better than wine.*

Clara touched her lips. How would it feel to kiss Jonah? She felt no such thing for Bishop

Silverman—far from it—but at least he belonged to their community.

In the rear-view mirror, Jonah's eyes found her again. That same quick smile followed. Saying nothing, Lydia rubbed his shoulder, which struck Clara with confusion. Her touch was more like a loved one's than a sister. Could their relationship still be a secret? But she had called him her brother, or had she lied?

Lydia looked back at Clara and kissed Jonah's cheek. "My poor brother looks worn out." She rubbed his shoulder again. "How's your shoulder from installing the fence? You said it had been bothering you."

"It's not bad," Jonah said.

Lydia took Clara's hand and placed it on Jonah's shoulder. "See how tight his muscles are? When they're like that, I rub liniment on them."

"She does a great job too," Jonah said. "It helps me get ready for another day of work." He worked his arm in a circle, and Clara could feel the muscles tightening and relaxing in her palm.

Let him kiss me with the kisses of his mouth: for thy love is better than wine.

Clara jerked her hand back, and Lydia patted Jonah's shoulder again. "And here I was, thinking someone could take my place with your massages."

Clasping her hands in her lap, Clara said

nothing. Whatever game Lydia was playing, she wanted no part of it. Thank goodness she had moved back home a few days ago.

Jonah pulled off the main road onto their road. "Clara, have you given any thought to putting up a stand in Clarksville and selling eggs and vegetables like Lydia suggested? Your garden looks great, and you mentioned having more than you need for canning."

Glad to be on a different subject, Clara nodded. "I'd like to do that."

"Vernon told me Alison was thinking about selling baskets in town. Maybe you two could share my tent."

Lydia opened the glove compartment and took out a phone. "Jonah's been telling me I should get a new phone. This one has a year's worth of minutes on it. What if I give it to you so you can call Alison about selling together?"

After Edna's spider bite, and until Clara learned to drive, she desperately needed a phone in case something similar happened again. "Thank you. That's very kind."

Lydia swiped a fingertip across the screen. "I'll put Vernon's and Alison's numbers in it when you can tell me. When I get home, I'll order a phone. Then I'll put all my numbers in it and delete them from this one." She returned the phone to the glove compartment. "I'll leave Jonah's number in it."

Clara wondered why Lydia hadn't offered to leave *her* number in it. Like the English sometimes said: *whatever*.

Chapter 8

Sitting in the shade of the tent Jonah had set up in Clarksville, in a grassy spot beside the sidewalk near a local store, Clara watched him drive away. Beside her, Alison raised the sleeve of her dress, the same sky-blue color as Clara's, and flexed her muscle. "My goodness, I wish *my* neighbor had muscles like that."

Clara shook her head. Some people thought the Amish and the Mennonites were perfect and never did things they shouldn't. They were human like anyone else, like Alison talking about men. Ignoring her friend's comment, she waved a fly away from one of the baskets of tomatoes on their table.

"Ignore me all you want," Alison said. "If Jonah joined our community, I'm sure you would pay more attention to him than you're doing now, especially since you say Lydia is his sister and not his fiancé."

Still unsure about Jonah and Lydia's relationship, Clara faced Alison. "If you paid as much attention to putting your baskets in a neat row on this table instead of talking about men, you might sell some."

"It was nice of Lydia to give you her phone. Now we can talk more." Alison's expression grew solemn. "How have you been, Clara? Except for when I kept John and Edna so you could plant your garden, I haven't seen you since the funeral. I was sorry to hear about Edna's spider bite and … well … you losing your baby. I prayed and prayed for God to bring you peace."

Clara appreciated her best friend. Alison might tease, but she never failed to show genuine concern when a problem arose. "I'm doing as well as I can. The garden keeps me busy, the children and canning vegetables too. John can wear holes in the knees of his pants as soon as I patch them."

"It was nice of Lydia to keep them for you today."

"How are your three boys? I'm sure Samuel has them working on something."

"They're weeding the garden. It's grown too big to get the tractor between the rows."

A couple stopped on the sidewalk to admire Clara's tomatoes and one of Alison's intricately woven baskets. Money passed hands and they went on their way, talking about how good fresh tomato sandwiches would taste for supper that night.

A woman with long, black hair and black eyes stopped a minute later. Clara admired her height. She stood at least six inches taller than both her and Alison. She was beautiful too, slender like a cattail. Clara noticed hearing aids in both ears. The woman bought a basket of tomatoes, wished Clara and Alison well, and left for her car parked in the lot behind the tent. Although Clara understood her words, which sounded as if they were said more in her throat than in her mouth, she had listened carefully to make sure.

Alison grabbed her arm. "Clara, that's Eliza Andrews! She's a famous artist. She lives right here in Clarksville. Can you imagine that?"

Clara had never heard of her. "Is she really that good?"

Alison's mouth fell open. "She's amazing! She was Amish and fell in love with her sign language teacher who lives here. Her family left the Amish in Ohio and moved here to be with her. How can you not know her?"

To wear hearing aids and use sign language, the woman must've been deaf or partially deaf. That must explain the way her words sounded. "This is the first time I've heard of her," Clara said. "That's how."

"Well, that makes sense. Samuel and I went to one of her art shows here a while back. Someone said she lost her first child and it almost ended her marriage. She and her husband—his name is Denver—managed to work through it. They have a family now. Isn't true love amazing?"

Clara turned toward the table. Of course true love was amazing. She knew that from her marriage to Abram.

Three more customers bought either baskets or tomatoes or both. On the street beside the sidewalk, vehicles passed, and some of the drivers turned their heads in curiosity. Clara didn't mind. They might not understand how she and Alison—beneath their blue dresses, pinned hair, and white kapps—were people too, but they were.

To her right, a huge truck pulled an enclosed trailer up the street's incline. The engine sounded like a cat's purr, but loud enough to fill her ears. Black smoke poured from the exhaust; its bitter smell made Clara wrinkle her nose. Inside the truck, the driver smiled and waved. She waved back, and Alison shoved her. "Look at you, waving at that English man. You're just as bad as me."

"I'm just being nice," Clara said. "The Bible says to love our neighbors the same as we love ourselves."

Alison twirled a lock of blonde hair that had escaped her kapp. "Does that count for Jonah too? As much as he helps you, it makes me wonder if he has feelings for you."

Clara said nothing. Since Alison had brought up the subject of Jonah, maybe she could answer a question or three. "Do you know what happened to Lydia's arm?"

"I've never met her," Alison said. "What's wrong with it?"

"It's her left arm. It's bent at a strange angle at the elbow. There's a scar on the inside of her elbow too. She said she had an accident but didn't say how when I asked about it."

Alison pursed her lips, a habit she had when something puzzled her. "Hmm, that *is* strange, almost as strange as how we thought she was Jonah's fiancé instead of his sister." Alison pursed her lips again. "Did I tell you that? I don't remember."

Clara didn't remember either. It was just something she assumed. The curiosity of it made her curious about something else. "What's this about Bishop Silverman's wife divorcing him? I *do* remember you telling me that."

Alison's eyes widened. "I *did* tell you that. Samuel's cousin—he lives where the bishop used to live—told us last fall when he visited. I started to ask more, but Samuel told me it was none of my affair and to not repeat it. It's funny how some men gossip when they're standing around, and then they tell us not to."

Clara agreed. Their men were supposed to rule the home, but they could make poor decisions like anyone else. She and Abram had talked everything through, and she loved him even more for it.

Coming up the incline in the street, a car caught her eye. Smiling, Bishop Silverman waved and pulled into the lot to park.

Alison patted Clara's shoulder. "That's quite a smile from our mysterious bishop. Maybe he'd like to make you his next wife."

Clara pushed Alison's hand away. "Behave. That story about his wife could just be an ugly rumor. She could've died like Abram." The thought gave Clara pause. If the bishop's wife had died, he understood how it felt to lose a loved one. He had always been kind to Clara, even bringing cabbage soup that time, plus seeds for her garden and facilitating their small community's contribution of money to help with her necessities.

The bishop left his car and came over. "Good morning, ladies." Looking over the tomatoes and baskets, he rubbed his hands together. "My garden is playing out, and I need some tomatoes."

Alison pushed one of her baskets toward the bishop. "They taste better in one of my baskets."

Clara covered her mouth to hide a grin. Regardless, a snicker escaped her tightened lips.

The bishop cut his eyes toward Alison. "You're always the joker. Well, the Bible says laughter is like a medicine.

Alison nodded. "While you two take your medicine, I need to visit the store for a moment."

She left for the variety store whose parking lot the bishop had parked in. When she got out of earshot, the bishop faced Clara. "I hope you don't mind me asking, but have you given any thought to how long you'll take for your mourning period? Some doctrine says up to two years."

Clara considered the question. The money from their community was coming in handy for the few bills she had, such as for chicken feed and the electricity for the water pump for the indoor plumbing. Along with the vegetables she already had, this year's crop would easily replace what she and the children had eaten since Abram had died. Although she hadn't learned how to drive either the tractor or the pickup truck, Jonah offered to take her wherever she needed to go. Since she thought the bishop had asked about her mourning period because he might be interested in courting her, and since she was in good shape financially, she wasn't in a hurry to court anyone. Besides, it had only been a few months since Abram had died. She tapped a fingertip to her lips. "What does *our* doctrine say about a mourning period?"

The bishop shrugged. "Some bishops think they should make all the decisions. I happen to think a woman's opinion should be considered."

Clara's current opinion, since she had decided to give up on Jonah, was to take as long as she wanted. "I think two years is fine for me."

The bishop's mouth worked as if he were a fish out of water. "That long?"

The disappointment in his voice amused Clara. She might consider courting him—it wasn't like she could court Jonah—and she had given up on marrying for love anyway. It would also give her a chance to find out if the rumor about the bishop's wife divorcing him were true. "Yes," she said, "that long."

"Really? Two whole years?"

Clara couldn't take it any longer. She burst out laughing, and the bishop—she really should call him Vernon now that he was making his intentions known—crossed his arms. "Laughter may be like a medicine," he said seriously, "but I don't understand what's so funny."

"It's not that you're funny," Clara said. "It's just that you're not very subtle. If I understand correctly, you want to know how long I'll mourn because you'd like to court me. Is that the case?"

Vernon's cheeks reddened. "Well, I didn't care to blurt it out."

Out of nowhere, the reality of Abram's death crashed in on Clara: his body lying beneath the hay loft door, his head twisted at such an unnatural angle, her screams as the realization that she had lost the love of her life washing over her like a shroud. She held her shoulders back, firm in her conviction. "Unless something drastically changes, I'll mourn the full two years. I apologize for laughing. After losing Abram so tragically, I'm surprised I don't cry myself to sleep every night."

"I'm sorry if I upset you," Vernon said softly. "I've come to care about you a great deal." He looked away and back. "I hate to ask, but if you wait the full two years, would you consider courting me then? I would ask your father, of course."

"Two years is a long time, Vernon. We'll have to see."

Alison left the store and joined them again. "Did anything happen while I was gone?"

Vernon whirled toward her. "What do you mean?"

"I meant did we get any more customers. What do you think I mean?"

"I … uh …"

"No," Clara said, "we didn't get any customers." She offered Vernon a basket of tomatoes. "Unless you're ready to pay for these."

"Oh, yes, thank you, Clara." He paid for the tomatoes. "I was wondering when you might return to church. We're meeting in Alison's home this Sunday."

"That's right," Alison said to Clara. "I just haven't told you yet. I'm sure Jonah would give you a ride."

Vernon cleared his throat. "Actually, I was going to offer a ride."

"Oh," Alison said, eyeing him and then Clara. "I see."

The rumble of a diesel engine came from toward downtown Clarksville. Jonah parked in the lot and joined them. "How's it going, ladies?"

Alison grinned at him. "Clara's taking bids on a ride to church Sunday at my house. The bishop offered to take her."

"I don't mind giving her a ride," Jonah said. "If

no one has any objection, I'd like to attend church too."

On the way to Clarksville earlier, Jonah had told Clara about Lakefest again. One of the attractions was hot air balloons. She could imagine when they were deflated at the end of the day, and that's what Vernon looked like now.

"It's not necessary," he said, peering up at Jonah from beneath the wide brim of his straw hat.

Jonah, who towered over the shorter bishop, tilted his head to one side. "I don't help Clara because it's necessary, Vernon. I help her because she's a strong woman who's been through a lot and is overcoming it. She's willing to learn new things too, like driving a tractor and a pickup, and I admire her a great deal."

"Well, she hasn't learned those things yet. Besides, it's a man's place to do those things and a woman's place to do as we say."

"Not if I were married to her. Women should be respected instead of ordered around."

Beside Clara, Alison gave a little snort. "I better gather my baskets. It looks like a storm is coming."

"What storm?" Vernon stepped out from under the tent and looked up. "I don't see any clouds."

Clara gave him his basket of tomatoes. Although the sky was perfectly clear, she could see storm clouds brewing, and she needed to blow them away if she could. "Jonah doesn't understand our ways, Vernon, please forgive him. You can pick me and the children up Sunday for church." She faced Jonah. "I'm sure Vernon doesn't mind if you come. We'll have lunch after. Maybe Lydia would like to come. Then you can give me and the children a ride home after and save Vernon the drive."

"I don't mind," Vernon said.

"Neither do I," Jonah said. "Like Clara said, it'll save you the drive." He smiled, big and bright, and clapped Vernon on the shoulder. "Aren't we a pair, wanting to help Clara? I bet she's stronger than the both of us put together."

Cringing at the blow, Vernon worked his shoulder. "I don't know about being strong. It feels like you dislocated my shoulder." He faced Clara. "I'll see you Sunday." He tipped his hat to Alison. "Good afternoon, Alison. I'll see you Sunday too."

As he drove away, Jonah faced Alison. "Did Clara tell you about our fishing trip here? I think she enjoyed the lake."

"Really?" Alison asked, rolling her eyes at Clara. "Was it just you two? That sounds very romant—"

"It was me and the children and Lydia and Vernon too," Clara said, wishing her friend would hush.

Jonah took his phone from its belt holder,

swiped the screen a few times, and held the screen toward Alison. "I told Clara she should go to the beach sometime. This is a picture I took the last time Lydia and I went."

"Oh, I agree," Alison said, again rolling her eyes at Clara. "I'd love a romantic trip to the beach."

Clara felt like clapping Alison on the shoulder. They weren't supposed to be so outspoken, especially around the English. "Maybe one day I'll see the beach. What I need is to visit my parents in Pennsylvania before winter. I haven't seen them since Abram's funeral."

"I'm sure Vernon will take you," Jonah said, winking at Alison.

Another customer stopped for the last of the tomatoes. Relieved she had sold out, Clara bought Alison's last two baskets. "There, now we can go home." She didn't say the rest: *and I can get away from you teasing people and look forward to getting back to church on Sunday.*

Chapter 9

Outside Samuel and Alison's home the following Sunday, Clara said hello to the members of her community. Each said how nice it was to see her and the children again, and to let them know if she needed anything. At her side, Vernon welcomed them, sometimes smiling at Clara as if she were already his wife. She wasn't sure how she felt about his proposal to court her. Although he meant it because of how he intended to ask her father's permission, something didn't quite sit right with the story of his wife, in which no one knew if she had left him or if she had died. Clara thought the latter. Vernon, like most Amish men around women outside of the family, was a little reserved. When Clara considered this, she wondered how he would act if they were married. If the truth be known, she preferred Jonah's quick wit and how he always kept someone guessing at what he might say. If he and Lydia weren't siblings and they got married, she would never be bored.

The community only consisted of three couples, plus Vernon and Clara and the children. When the last couple, an elderly man and woman who had been happily married for sixty years, had stopped to welcome Clara and the children back, Vernon said they better go in. Curious as to why Jonah and Lydia weren't here, she seated the children and returned to the porch to wait.

Over the woods to the east, the sun warmed the late August morning. Samuel had mowed the lawn yesterday, leaving the aroma of cut grass in the front yard. Giving up on Jonah and Lydia, Clara went inside and joined the children on the sofa. Around the huge family room that doubled as a kitchen, people sat in rocking chairs and on wooden benches. Samuel and Alison, being the welcoming couple, had relinquished two easy chairs by the fireplace to the elderly couple, choosing instead two simple straight-back chairs beside the sofa.

Clara couldn't help but wonder about Jonah and Lydia. It wasn't like him to commit to something and not do it. Near the fireplace with his Bible, Vernon motioned her to come. When she did, he leaned close. "I got a text from Jonah while you were outside. Lydia had some kind of spell, so they couldn't come."

"A spell?" Clara whispered. "What kind of spell?"

"I don't know. Did she have any problems while you and the children stayed with them?"

"None at all."

"Well, we should keep them in our prayers. I'll go ahead with the service." As Vernon opened his Bible, Clara returned to the sofa. He welcomed the small congregation, then pointed out how happy everyone was about Clara and John and Edna's return. Vernon's usual monotone preaching style failed to keep Clara's attention. What could be wrong with Lydia? Other than her crooked arm, she had never shown any signs of a physical issue.

The first hour of the service passed slowly. John and Edna fidgeted but kept quiet. Around the room, most people nodded at certain lines from the Bible. When the two younger men nodded off to sleep, their wives nudged them.

By the end of the service two hours later, the women had stopped nudging their lightly snoring husbands. Clara understood the men perfectly. Even with the air conditioning, the warmth from so many people in one room made her drowsy as well.

At Vernon's final "Amen," the women set the

table with food, while the men talked about their gardens and their paying crops, such as wheat and soybeans. In the bathroom, Clara checked the phone Lydia had given her for a text from Jonah. Seeing none, she said a prayer for healing. Sister or not, fiancé or not, Amish or Mennonite or not, Lydia was a sister in Christ.

Someone knocked on the bathroom door. Clara opened it to reveal Alison. "Bishop Silverman just told me Lydia is sick. Did Jonah text you?"

"I thought he would because we expected him, but he hasn't."

"I hope Lydia's all right. I suppose the bishop will take you home after we eat."

Clara hadn't thought of that. "Yes, I suppose he will." If ever there was time she wished she knew how to drive, this, along with when the spider bit Edna, was one of them. As good as Jonah and Lydia had been to her, she would like to help if she could.

During the meal, Clara picked at her food and answered small talk from everyone who asked how she and the children were doing. Sitting beside her, Vernon smiled at her occasionally, which didn't go unnoticed by some of the people around the table. The reactions were divided between approving and disapproving glances, and Clara wondered how many of the disapproving glances were split between the rumor about his wife divorcing him and the fact that she was still in mourning over Abram's death.

Done with their food, the couples thanked Alison and Samuel for their hospitality, saying it was time for their Sunday afternoon nap and left. Clara helped Alison clear the remaining dishes. John and Edna went outside with Alison's boys, then came back in, saying it was too hot to play. Samuel and Vernon were finishing second helpings of peanut butter pie. Drying one of the dishes Alison had given her, Clara heard the unmistakable sound of a diesel pickup engine. Out in the driveway, visible through the window over the sink, Jonah pulled in and parked. Despite the temptation to run out and ask about Lydia, Clara finished drying the dish. Jonah left the truck and came toward the house. He knocked and stuck his head in. "Can I come in?"

Alison set a dish with a piece of pie on the table. "Only if you have dessert." She cut her eyes at Clara. "We were worried about you."

"And Lydia," Vernon said. "Since you're here, I assume she's better."

"She's asleep. She gets terrible migraine headaches; only sleep helps." Jonah came a few steps closer. "Thank you for the pie, Alison, but I should get back." He faced Clara. "Are you ready?"

John and Edna, who had joined Jonah, took one of his hands each. His tender smile warmed Clara's heart.

Vernon cleared his throat. "I was about to take Clara home."

Alison opened the door and looked out. "I don't see a cloud in the sky, but I think a storm's coming."

Vernon went to a window by the door and looked out. "I don't hear any thunder. How do you know a storm's coming?"

On the way back to the sink, Alison winked at Clara. "Oh, I just know these things." She filled several plates with food, put them in a box, and gave it to Clara. "There. Now you and your neighbors will have something for supper." She wrapped the slice of pie meant for Jonah and offered it to Vernon. "And you can have something to help you recognize when a storm is coming."

Samuel cut his eyes between Vernon and Alison, eventually settling on Vernon. "Please excuse my wife. After ten years of marriage, even *I* don't know where she gets some of her ideas."

Vernon took the pie. "Perhaps a firm hand would—"

Jonah took a single step toward Vernon. "I may not be from your community, but I know better than to resort to violence."

"He didn't mean that," Clara said. "It's just a figure of speech."

Samuel went to Jonah. "She's right, Jonah. Although our ways seem foreign to you, we don't believe in violence."

"I'm glad to hear that," Jonah said. "Unfortunately, I've heard stories of Amish and Mennonite men resorting to violence in the home." He eyed Vernon. "I doubt I need to explain what might happen if that ever happened to someone I care about, do I?"

Vernon paled. "I didn't mean how it sounded, Jonah. Please, we're friends. It's just a misunderstanding." He offered his hand. "All right?"

Jonah's huge hand engulfed Vernon's hand. Clara watched his forearm muscles tighten as he squeezed. At the very moment she expected to hear bones crack, he loosened his grip and beamed a smile. "Of course we're friends, Vernon. Thank you for clearing up our misunderstanding." He took the box from Clara. "Let's get you and the children home."

The thirty-minute drive passed silently. At her house, she told Jonah to wait. Once she got the children inside, she returned to the air-conditioned interior of the truck and faced him. "Why did you squeeze Vernon's hand so hard? You could've hurt him."

Jonah shrugged. "I have a firm handshake. It didn't bother him."

"You know what I mean."

Jonah removed his seatbelt and turned to face her. "Regardless of you defending him for his so-called figure of speech, anyone who talks about using a 'firm hand,' as he calls it, has a problem." Jonah paused. "It's obvious he's chosen you as his next wife, and I don't want—"

"How dare you," Clara said, heat flaring in her cheeks. "You're the one who forced us together on that fishing trip without telling me."

Jonah looked away. "I like Vernon. I even think he cares about you and the children." Jonah faced her again. "I'm sorry for how I acted. I just want you and the children to be happy."

Jonah's hand was on the console between the two seats. The temptation to slip her fingers into his overwhelmed Clara, but she had decided to shove her feelings for him aside. No good could come from losing the discipline she was fighting so hard to maintain. If she did, and if he returned her feelings, it would ruin their friendship, and she couldn't allow that to happen.

"You're quiet," Jonah said. "Please forgive me. Your friendship means more to me than I can say."

His soft and sincere tone touched Clara deeply. "I've never shown you Abram's grave. Let me check on the children, and then I will." She peeked into the door. Full from their lunch, John and Edna had fallen asleep on the sofa. At the truck again, she asked Jonah to follow her to the back of the house.

Beneath the huge oak, where sparse grass was attempting to grow through the wheat straw covering the red mound of soil, she stopped. A simple wooden cross, painted white, marked the head of the grave.

Jonah touched the tip of the cross. "You've got an amazing wife and family, Abram. I regret not getting to know you better. I think we would've been good friends."

A gentle breeze rustled the leaves overhead, reminding Clara of how she and Abram used to talk in bed at night about their plans for the farm. To keep Jonah from seeing her cry, she turned away. Abram had never known they were expecting the child she had lost. Maybe he was holding their son or daughter in Heaven at this very moment.

"Clara, do you want me to leave?"

The leaves rustled once more. The warm breeze kissed Clara's cheek as if it were Abram's lips. If only that tender touch were his blessing for her and Jonah to be together, as impossible as it seemed.

Wiping tears, she faced Jonah.

He reached for her. When his palm was almost cupping her cheek, he lowered his hand to his side. "It breaks my heart to see you so sad. I can't imagine losing someone you love so much." Jonah's kind voice, his tender gaze, his broad shoulders—all three were exactly like Abram's.

A sudden realization struck Clara: she might only be attracted to Jonah because he was so similar to Abram. If that were the case, and she certainly knew it was possible, it was wrong to have feelings for him based on her love for Abram. A person should be loved for the unique individual God made them, not because they were like someone else.

Regardless of her revelation, Jonah's brown eyes drew her to him. More than anything she wanted him to take her into his arms and tell her everything would be all right, that they would be together one day, that God's commandment to love one another were meant to cross the boundaries between English and her community.

As it had done so often lately, shame heated her cheeks. How dare she think such things. How dare she question her commitment to the Beachy Amish Mennonite way of life. How dare she turn her back on everything she and Abram believed in. To do so defiled her memory of him.

Standing as tall as possible, shoulders held back, chin raised in defiance to her feelings, she looked directly into Jonah's eyes. "I wanted to show you Abram's grave because I know you care about the children and I like he did. I value our friendship, and I appreciate everything you've done for us. I also know we still need your help in the future, like with wiring the house. Vernon has asked to court me. He also intends to ask my father, which is very respectful of him. Saying that, I'm in no hurry to court anyone. I need time to learn the difference between my love for Abram and my love for another person." At the pull of Jonah's brown eyes, Clara hesitated. "Whoever that person might be. Does that make sense?"

A third breeze rustled the oak leaves overhead. Jonah looked up at them and then returned to Clara. "I think Abram agrees. I'm happy to be a friend to you and the children, Clara. As far as your electrical work, when can I start?"

Clara paused. Such work would be expensive. To avoid blurring the lines of their friendship, she preferred to have the money before he started, but that would be a while yet. "I don't want to become a charity case for you, Jonah. Give me an estimate of the cost, and you can start when I have the money." She was tempted to offer her hand to shake as men did, but she knew his touch would melt her resolve. "Do we have a deal?"

"I'm not sure," Jonah said, crossing his arms. "How much should I charge for everything else I've done for you? We should get that out of the way before I do anything else, don't you think? Besides, if you intend to court Vernon, it won't be appropriate for him to drive you to visit your parents. That means I'll have to do it."

Despite her serious attitude of the moment, Clara laughed. "Oh, so you'll *have* to do it. You make it sound like such a chore."

"Not if you pay me well. What's it worth to you? Gas for the drive to Pennsylvania and back isn't cheap. I'm sure I can't sleep in your parent's home, so I'll need money for a hotel room while we're there."

Clara crossed her arms too. Jonah hadn't returned her laugh, so she didn't know if he were teasing her or not. Still, since she wanted the relationship to be friendly instead of romantic, she should pay him for his efforts. "What if you write down a running bill? Then I can pay you along the way."

Tilting his head side to side, Jonah rolled his eyes. "Mmm, I'll have to think about it. I think you owe me around a thousand dollars so far." He knelt to pick up a small quartz rock from Abram's grave and offered it to Clara. "Take that and give it back."

Regardless of her confusion at his request, Clara did so. "Now what?"

Jonah pocketed the rock. "Consider that your first payment. By the time I wire your house, teach you to drive your tractor and truck, and take you to Pennsylvania, I'll be able to retire from selling rocks."

"Fine. Just make sure to keep a record of what I owe you. Shouldn't you get back to Lydia? How long has she had those headaches?"

"A while. Her therapist—I mean her doctor—said stress could cause them."

Clara wondered why Jonah had changed "therapist" to "doctor," plus what kind of stress Lydia would have out in the country. Yet another mystery about Lydia, along with her arm and her and Jonah's relationship, had presented itself.

She walked Jonah to his truck and told him she would let him know when she wanted to go to Pennsylvania. Knowing Vernon wouldn't approve of him driving her, she told Jonah she would explain her reasoning: that if she and Vernon courted in the future, it might not seem appropriate to their community.

As Jonah drove away, Clara considered what her parents would think of her driver. The Amish often hired the English to drive them on long trips, so it shouldn't be a problem. Still, parents were parents, and they might notice how her and Jonah, no matter how much she tried to hide it, were more than mere friends.

Chapter 10

In the kitchen, having finished canning the last of the green beans, Clara flipped the calendar beside the icebox. Today was the first of September, and John's birthday was this Saturday, the third. Something about this time of year had felt different, and this was it. No doubt she had forgotten because Abram usually kept up with the family's birthdays.

She went to Edna at the table, where she was drying several canning jars that would be used for another crop of tomatoes in a few days. Regardless of the Amish custom of having a quiet gathering for family birthdays, Clara liked to include her daughter in the decision about John. Since he was feeding the chickens, it would be a good time to plan something.

"Edna, I forgot your brother's birthday. He'll be four on Saturday. What should we do for him?"

Edna stopped drying the jar. "When's my birthday, Mama?"

"Yours was three weeks ago. You turned five, remember? Jonah and Lydia brought ice cream."

Edna licked her lips. "Banana ice cream too."

"That's right, but John's favorite is strawberry."

"Can Jonah and Lydia make some?"

The thought had crossed Clara's mind, but she wanted to invite Vernon to supper to explain how Jonah would drive her and the children to Pennsylvania in two weeks. "I'm going to ask Vernon to supper. We'll have strawberry cake instead. I'll ask him to bring some from the grocery store."

Drying another jar, Edna stopped and looked up at Clara. "You smile at Jonah more than anyone else. He's more like Papa than anyone else too. Why can't you marry him?"

The question surprised Clara. Her observant daughter must've been watching her and Jonah quite a bit. "Well, sweetheart," she said, patting Edna's back, "our Ordnung forbids marriage between us and English men."

Edna set the jar aside. "Bishop Silberman isn't nice like Papa was. Will you marry him?"

Clara smiled. Edna sometimes confused her V and B sounds. "I don't know who I'll marry. Bishop

Silverman and I may court one day. We'll see how it goes. Are you excited to visit Grandma and Grandpa?"

"I don't remember them very much."

"That's why we're going to see them. We'll see your papa's mama and papa too." Clara stood from the table. "The jars are dry enough. Let's tell John about his birthday Saturday and Bishop Silverman coming. Then we'll wash up and decide what we want for supper tonight."

* * *

Saturday morning, Clara woke to rain pattering on the tin roof of the house. Through the space between the raised window and the sill, the watery aroma of the rain blew in with the breeze. On mornings like this, before John and Edna came along, she and Jonah would—

No. To think of those times made her think of Jonah more than Abram. It was almost as if her sweet husband were trying to force his memories from her mind and replace them with thoughts of Jonah.

She rolled to her back. In the center of the huge bed, she felt like a single leaf in the middle of the lake at Clarksville, alone and sinking within the whirlpool of her life. Vernon would never win her love, but she had to try—if not for her sake, for the children's sake. What if someone else came along, such as a Beachy Amish Mennonite man as tender and caring as Abram, who would be happy to live on this farm, far from their community near Nathalie? Could she learn to love him?

Clara flung the sweat-dampened sheet to the side. During the long summer without air conditioning like at Alison's home, she had taken to sleeping in one of Abram's shirts to at least keep her legs cooler.

The rain pattered the tin roof harder. The breeze gusted through the window, flaring the curtains and cooling her legs. She kissed her fingertips and raised them toward the ceiling: a kiss good morning to her beloved Jonah.

Gritting her teeth in anger, Clara got out of bed and dressed.

She would *not* think of Jonah when she meant to think of Abram. How could she betray her sweet husband in such a way?

Choosing to remain barefooted in her blue dress, she checked John and Edna. Both were still dreaming the innocent and uncomplicated dreams of children.

After splashing through puddles in the yard for eggs, then doing the same to milk the cow, she washed her feet in the bathtub and returned to the kitchen to make pancakes and plan John's birthday supper.

As she measured flour into a bowl, vehicle tires splashed in the driveway. Not expecting anyone, she looked through the screened door. Lydia got out of her car and hurried to the porch with a large bowl. Clara opened the door for her and offered her a dishtowel to dry the rain from her face. Lydia set the bowl on the table. "Jonah said today was John's birthday. We know how he loves strawberry ice cream from when you stayed with us, so I brought you some from our freezer." She took the cover off the bowl. Inside the bowl of strawberries sat a smaller bowl of blueberries. "We know how he likes blueberry pancakes too, so I brought these." Wiping her face, she took a few steps toward the center of the kitchen. "This is the first time I've been here. I love how large the room is."

Clara admired Lydia's stylish haircut that revealed the nape of her neck. Hair like that wouldn't need to be pinned up every morning and hidden with a kapp. She couldn't, however, admire her crooked left arm, but it hadn't seemed to bother her any, both when Clara had stayed with her and Jonah and when Lydia had just brought the bowls inside.

At the wood stove, Lydia pointed at it. "I'm sure that feels wonderful in the winter." She turned to face Clara. "What do you think of Jonah—as a friend, I mean? He's a wonderful person, isn't he?"

The question confused Clara. Whether Lydia was Jonah's sister or fiancé, she should know if he were a wonderful person or not. Clara ignored the question. "Thank you for the berries." She got two bowls from a cupboard and poured the berries into them, rinsed and dried the empty ones and offered them to Lydia. "Now you can take them home."

Lydia didn't take the bowls. "I understand Amish and Mennonite women don't like to be alone with a man. How does it make you feel when you're alone with Jonah?"

Clara set the bowls on the table. "I value his friendship."

"But how do you feel about him?" Lydia leaned her backside against the table and crossed her ankles. "I'm a woman, you can tell me."

Clara noted how Lydia hadn't said she was Jonah's sister, just that she was a woman. Sister or not, what kind of game was she playing? She offered the bowls again. "As helpful as he is, he makes me feel like his sister. You know how that feels, don't you?"

Just the hint of a smile—knowing or not—passed across Lydia's lips. "Oh, I know how a lot of things feel." She took the bowls. "I also know how some people feel about each other. It doesn't take a sister to see that kind of thing." At the door, she faced Clara again. "Like I see how Vernon feels about you."

"You're right," Clara said, hoping to end Lydia's suggestion that more than friendship existed between her and Jonah. "In fact, Vernon is coming to John's birthday supper tonight."

Lydia nodded and said she hoped the supper went well. At the sound of her car leaving, Clara dropped into one of the chairs at the table. Not only did Lydia seem to think there was more than friendship between Jonah and her, it seemed as if she approved of it. Clara stood. Regardless, she needed to make breakfast and plan John's birthday supper. At the rate the day was passing, Vernon would be here before she knew it.

* * *

Fresh from a bath after a warm afternoon of cooking, Clara toweled her hair as dry as possible and pinned it up. A clean blue dress and kapp followed. She had already bathed John and Edna, who were playing quietly in the living area of the kitchen.

Standing in front of the full-length mirror on the back of the bedroom door, Clara turned around. Abram used to tease her about her petite size, calling her his little dragonfly, meaning she was small, while her hair reminded him of the fire a dragon was supposed to breathe. Not wanting to go barefoot or wear her everyday shoes, she put on a pair of leather sandals Abram used to like and went to the kitchen. In the far corner near their toy box, Edna and John turned around. "When can we eat?" Edna asked.

"Me too," John said. "My stomach is mad."

Edna giggled. "It's not mad when it growls, silly. It means it's hungry."

John pushed his lips out in a pout. "Be nice. It's my birthday."

"I agree," Clara said. "Let's set the table. Bishop Silverman should be here soon."

Edna brought silverware to the table. "Sometimes you call him Vernon. Why is that?"

"He asked me to call him that when we went fishing with Jonah and Lydia, remember?" Clara took four glasses to the table, and John moved them to the placemats.

"Is he your boyfriend?" he asked. "I hope not. He's not like Papa. Jonah's like Papa."

Clara went to the cupboard for dishes. Although John was now four, he was entirely too smart for his age. That's what she got for reading to him and Edna every night before bed.

The children's foreheads beaded with sweat from the wood cookstove's heat. Air conditioning would be nice, but a propane gas stove would make cooking much simpler. Not as much wood would have to be bought during the winter, with none during the summer. Clara went to the stove to check the chicken casserole in the oven. The gravy bubbled. The meat was browning. The carrots, peas, and celery smelled wonderful. She closed the door and stirred the green beans in a pot on top, checked the boiling potatoes and stirred them too.

A vehicle horn beeped outside. For a moment, Clara thought it was Vernon, but the horn sounded different. At the door, she gawked. A truck from the home improvement store in South Boston was backing up to the door. Clara ran out to the driver's side door and waved until he stopped and rolled the window down. "What are you doing?" she asked. "I haven't ordered anything."

The driver looked at a sheet of paper. "Are you Clara Engelman?"

"I am, but—"

"Are you sure you didn't order anything? It's been paid for."

"Who paid for it? Wait, what is it?"

"It's a propane stove."

The first thing that popped into Clara's mind was Jonah had bought the stove. The second thing was how she didn't have a propane tank.

At the end of the driveway, a truck pulled in

with a propane tank on the back. The driver pulled up to the house and rolled the window down. "Are you Clara Engelman?"

Before she could answer, Vernon came up the driveway and got out, a bouquet of flowers in his hand. "Well, well. It looks like someone's getting a new stove."

Clara went to him. He must've bought the stove since he knew what was in the first truck. "Vernon, I appreciate this, but it's too much."

He shook the flowers. "How can flowers be too much?" He returned to the car and brought out a wrapped present. "I got a little something for John."

"You didn't buy the stove?"

Vernon shrugged. "It would've made a nice wedding present, but we aren't even courting yet." He took off his hat and ran his fingers through his hair. "You mean you don't know who bought it?"

Since Vernon hadn't bought the stove, Clara still thought Jonah had, but she didn't want such an extravagant gift to upset Vernon. "I know," she said. "I bought it last month and forgot about it."

John opened the screened door. "Did that big truck bring my present?"

"It's a present for all of us," Clara said.

At the tailgate of the first truck, one man lowered

a lift while the other asked Clara to sign a form saying she had received the stove. Flustered to no end, she scribbled her name. "You'll have to put it in the barn. I forgot it was coming today, and I'm not ready to put it in the kitchen."

The man with the propane tank offered her another form. "Where do you want the tank?"

"In the barn." Clara scribbled her name. "I'll have someone connect it to the stove later."

The man folded the paper and shoved it into his pocket. "Make sure the installer is qualified. Gotta be safe, you know." He backed the truck toward the barn. A second man got out to help him put the tank inside. When that truck left, the men with the stove unloaded it into the barn and drove away too.

Edna peered through the screen door. "Mama, I think the casserole is burning."

Clara rushed inside. Bitter smelling smoke was seeping from the oven door. Using oven mitts to protect her hands from the hot container, she took the casserole out and placed it on the stovetop.

Vernon came over. "Hmm, it's black as soot. Do you usually cook it that long?" With her mouth hanging open, Clara whirled toward him. "He offered the flowers. "I'm just teasing, Clara. Maybe we can scrape the black part off."

John came over. "Is my present something to eat? We can't eat that, and I'm hungry."

Steam rose from the boiling green beans and potatoes. Clara moved them to a side table before they burned too. She put the flowers in a vase and took them to the supper table. Dropping into a chair, she didn't know whether to laugh or cry. She appreciated whoever had bought the stove, but their timing was terrible.

Vernon and the children came over and sat too. He gave John the present. "Happy birthday, young man."

John ripped the paper open. "Look, Mama, it's a book about fire engines."

Edna giggled. "We almost needed a *real* fire engine."

Clara's eyes filled with tears. Vernon stood. "Come now, Clara, there's always a silver lining in every cloud. Let's go out to eat. What would you like?"

She took a napkin from the holder and wiped her eyes. "What would you like, John? It's your birthday, so you choose."

"I want peetzer."

Edna poked his arm. "It's pizza."

"That's what I said."

"Did not."

"Did too."

"Now, now," Vernon said.

Clara closed her eyes. If Jonah bought that stove, she was going to thank him—then kill him. She stood. "All right, pizza it is."

"Yay!" John and Edna screamed.

Vernon frowned. "Pizza gives me heartburn."

"Do you need a fire engine?" Edna asked.

Clara dropped to the chair again. She had heard of Amish and Mennonites who sometimes drank alcohol. If some were single mothers with a man trying to court them, she understood why.

* * *

At home again, after Vernon had graciously taken everyone for pizza regardless of his heartburn, Clara spooned the strawberry ice cream Lydia had brought into four bowls. Edna took them to the table, John said a short blessing, and Vernon patted his back. "That's a good boy, John. Happy birthday, Son."

John didn't say anything, and Clara knew why: Abram had told John that very thing on his last birthday, and the memory made him miss his papa. Everyone ate silently. Vernon's comment made Clara miss Abram too. If she told the truth, unlike when she had shamefully lied about buying the propane stove, she didn't care for Vernon calling John "Son" either. They hadn't even started courting yet, and the comment made Clara feel like he was trying to take Abram's place already.

The children yawned between spoons of ice cream. When they finished, Clara reminded them to thank Vernon for everything. Then she had them brush their teeth, say their prayers, and got them into bed.

Returning to the kitchen, she was surprised to see Vernon washing the bowls. This was a woman's job when one was in the home. Saying nothing, she dried them and put them away.

He gave her the last bowl. "I didn't even think about you washing them. I guess I've gotten used to doing my own housework at home."

Clara understood the note of sadness in his voice. They both had lost their spouses, his possibly from a divorce, and it was a lonely burden to bear. "What was your wife like?" she asked, facing him.

"I'm sure you've heard the rumors of her leaving me, but she passed away. I don't understand how people can be so cruel."

"I agree," Clara said, meaning it. "They even say she divorced you."

Vernon shared a soft smile. "I'm glad that's just a rumor. If an Amish or Mennonite couple divorces, they're still married in God's eyes, so they can't marry again."

The implication was plain to Clara: if his wife had divorced him, he couldn't take Abram's place.

She asked him to join her in the living area. She sat in a rocking chair. He sat on the sofa.

"You're a very sensible woman," he said. "To avoid any sense of impropriety, you won't join me on the sofa."

"We do the best we can, Vernon. Thank God for his forgiveness." Clara paused. She needed to tell Vernon about Jonah driving her and the children to see her parents in two weeks, and this was the perfect time to do so. "You know I haven't seen my parents since the funeral. I've asked Jonah to drive me and the children in two weeks. I hope you won't mind."

"Not at all," Vernon said, sincerity in his voice. "I suppose you know I'd like to court you. If you allow it, your parents might think it improper for me to drive you, and I don't want to risk my standing as a bishop. Will you tell them about me when you go?"

So there it was, him openly admitting his intention to court her. She could see no reason not to. "I can."

"Have you decided how long your mourning period will last?"

Clara hesitated. She didn't like being pushed, and it felt like Vernon was pushing her. "I'm not sure. It's only been six months since Abram died."

Vernon's mouth twitched. "You could ask your

father."

"I ... I suppose." Again, the feeling of being trapped in a whirlpool engulfed Clara. She would never love Vernon. Yes, he was a kind and decent man, but something about him confused her. She would rather marry a man she loved—one like Jonah. She bit her lower lip. How many times must she tell herself to stop thinking of Jonah romantically? They would never be together, and that was that.

Rubbing his hands together, Vernon stood. "I'm glad we got that settled. If everything works out with your parents, we might be married in no time. Thank you for inviting me to John's birthday supper. I feel like a genuine member of the family already. Goodnight."

Clara stepped out on the porch as he drove away. Although he was right about him driving her to Pennsylvania risking his standing as a bishop, what about her standing as a Beachy Amish Mennonite woman and mother? Also, the children would've been with them, so why was he so concerned about his standing? Could he really be hiding something about his wife?

Above her, millions of stars twinkled in the night sky. To remind herself of Abram's arms around her, she wrapped her own arms around herself, but her thin arms couldn't begin to ward off the cool September air like her dear husband's arms had so many times before.

Since she didn't believe she would ever love Vernon, maybe God would allow a miracle and have her father disapprove of the courtship so soon.

The crisp night air drew her to the driveway, or perhaps it drew her to the lights in the windows of Jonah's home over the hill. A better miracle would be for Jonah to walk over that hill and pledge his love to her.

Clara held her face in her hands and wept.

Such a thing would never happen. She would end up in a loveless marriage on her part, doomed to living out the long and lonely years of her life as nothing more than the wife of someone instead of the dream of someone.

In the house again, she walked the rooms, recalling memories of Abram. Here was the rocking chair he made. Here was the corner desk where he wrote his plans for the farm. Here was the pillow he slept on.

She picked it up and held it to her nose. No, the washing and scrubbing had removed his scent like Vernon was trying to remove her husband's love from Clara's heart, but she would never allow that to happen as long as she lived.

Chapter 11

Yawning in the front seat of Jonah's truck, Clara couldn't wait to get out and stretch her legs from the long drive to Pennsylvania. By the LED clock on the truck's dash, they had been on the road over seven hours, some of that from traffic around Washington, D.C. At least John and Edna would whisper in her ear every so often when they needed a bathroom, which allowed for a break from the endless miles. Jonah straightened in the seat and worked his shoulders. "Whew, I'm bushed. At least Pennsylvania's closer than Ohio."

Clara recalled how Lydia's relatives lived in Ohio. "Does Lydia drive to Ohio often?"

"Not since the last time." Jonah glanced at her. "Don't the Amish and Mennonites have rules about being nosy?"

"What do you mean?"

"You seem curious about Lydia."

Clara faced the passenger door window. Yes, she was nosy, but she didn't like Jonah calling her nosy. Regardless, while she was being nosy, she could be nosy about something else. She turned to face him. "I'm really enjoying my new propane stove you installed for me. The kitchen doesn't get as hot as it did with the woodburning stove."

"But you kept that for heat."

"Only until you install the wiring and the heat pump. Will you buy that too?"

"What do you mean?" Jonah asked, narrowing his eyes at her. "I thought you bought it."

"Oh, I'm just teasing." Clara didn't care for lying—she would have to pray for forgiveness before bed tonight—but who in the world had bought that stove?

Ten minutes later they entered the small town of Buck, where Jonah had reserved a hotel room. He soon took a right and drove into the countryside. Oak and maple leaves were turning from green to yellow, orange, and red. Beside the road to the right, a fence made of white-painted boards surrounded a small herd of Black Angus beef cattle grazing in ankle-deep grass. Jonah said he wanted to raise that breed for their delicious steaks. He lowered the driver's side window. "What do you smell, Clara?"

"I smell poop," Edna said, and John giggled.

"I smell a way to earn a living," Jonah said. Using a button on his left armrest, he lowered Clara's window. "How about it, Clara? What do you smell?"

Grinning, she looked back at Edna and John. "One, two, three, what do we smell?"

"Poop!" they all yelled. Then they laughed hysterically, including Jonah.

Like so many other wonderful moments with him, this one reminded her of similar moments with Abram, which was how she and the children knew to yell "Poop!" at the same time.

"I love hearing y'all laugh," Jonah said. "It makes me feel like a kid again."

Clara agreed. Laughing with her children made her feel like a kid again too. Sadly, though, since she and Jonah could never be more than friends, her mood darkened like the trundling black clouds of a thunderstorm on a sultry summer afternoon back home in Virginia. Yes, he was kind and helpful and fun to be with. The children liked him too, so why couldn't a Beachy Amish Mennonite man come along with those same qualities? Then she might marry for love instead of for convenience, like if she married Vernon.

A few more miles passed. The truck's GPS

system said they would arrive at their destination in one mile. Clara could soon see the tin roof of the two-story house tucked within an oak grove. The red siding was much darker than the oak leaves, changing from green to orange.

When Jonah pulled into the gravel driveway, where two trucks and two cars were parked, Clara's parents, Aaron and Lena came out onto the porch. At age fifty, their hair was turning from brown to gray. Aaron, or Papa as Clara called him, wore dark pants, a gray shirt, and black suspenders. Unlike most Amish, he kept his beard neatly trimmed. Like most Amish, he kept no moustache. Lena, or Mama as Clara called her, wore a blue dress and a white kapp.

Behind them came Clara's brother and sister, Alfred and Susan, who resembled younger versions of Mama and Papa. Of their parent's three children, Clara was the youngest.

From behind Alfred and Susan came Rebecca, Alfred's wife, and Daniel, Susan's husband. Jonah had left Virginia early, so Alfred and Susan's six children each were still in school.

As Jonah parked, Clara's family gathered near the front of the truck. Clara got out and stretched her back. "What a long drive."

John and Edna got out and stood by her. Mama knelt in front of them. "How are my youngest grandchildren? We have lunch ready if you're hungry."

Jonah raised the cover on the bed of his truck, took out two suitcases, and went to Clara, who faced her relatives. "This is Jonah, my neighbor I told you about."

Mama stood. "How kind of you to drive Clara all the way up here."

"Not to mention helping her when the spider bit Edna," Papa said.

Clara hadn't told them about losing the baby. They would just worry, and she didn't want that. She hadn't even told John and Edna. Jonah—sweet and kind Jonah—had asked the doctors to keep the baby's tiny body in case she wanted to bury it beside Abram, which they had done one morning while the children were still asleep at his house.

"I'm just glad I was there to help," Jonah said to Papa.

Edna grabbed Jonah's hand with both of hers. Not to be outdone, John grabbed his other hand. Mama and Papa looked at each other. "Well," Papa said, "it looks like my grandchildren are quite attached to you."

"Very much so," Susan said. "You all look like you were made for each other."

Of all of her family, Susan was Clara's favorite.

Like her, Susan had married for love instead of convenience, like Alfred had. Still, he and Rebecca seemed to have grown to love each other over the years.

"Would you like some lunch?" Susan asked Jonah.

Jonah thanked her and said he didn't want to intrude. He took the suitcases to the porch and came back. "I better get to town and check into my hotel. "Clara, just give me a call when you'd like to leave."

She followed him to the truck and held the door as he started to close it. "You're welcome to lunch. They wouldn't ask if they didn't mean it." Losing her train of thought because of his intense brown eyes, she looked down and then back up. "I want you to stay too. Please say you will."

Jonah's eyes cut toward her family. "They sure are watching us," he said, keeping his voice down. "I don't want them to get the wrong idea."

As much as Clara hated to agree, she did. "I suppose you're right. I'll call you later and see how you are."

As she joined her family, Jonah backed the truck into the road and drove away.

Everyone went inside. Susan, whose freckles must number in the hundreds, held Clara's arm to keep her a few steps behind. "My goodness," she whispered. "You didn't tell me your neighbor was so handsome. I want to hear all about him after lunch."

"He's not Beachy Amish Mennonite," Clara hissed. "That's all you need to know."

Susan tugged Clara toward a corner of the large, combined kitchen and living area. "You're much prettier than me. You could convert Jonah if you wanted to. Don't you want to? I would if I were you. Don't you want to?"

Tempted to laugh at her vivacious sister, whose flaming red curls peeked from beneath her kapp, Clara shoved her away instead. "Behave before Mama or Papa hears. They'd question me to no end if they thought I loved an English man."

"Oh, please," Susan said, grinning mischievously. "I saw how you ran after him when he went to his truck. I don't blame you. His pretty eyes made me want to run after him too."

Mama waved them over. "Come and eat. You two can catch up later."

Clara sat between John and Edna. Papa said the blessing, making sure to thank God for Clara and John and Edna arriving safely, plus thanking Him for her helpful neighbor, Jonah.

Plates were filled with steaming helpings of meat loaf, mashed potatoes, sweet peas, and homemade rolls. Bites of each were followed with swallows of ice-cold apple cider, sweet and tangy.

Mama remarked at how John and Edna had grown since she last saw them, adding how she would love to see them more often. Clara recognized Mama's regretful tone, the same as when she and Abram had told the family they were moving to Virginia. Like Mama, Papa and Alfred had mirrored that regret back then, while Susan had said there was nothing wrong with experiencing new places and meeting new people.

Papa sipped cider and lowered the glass. "Now that you have nothing to keep you in Virginia, why don't you sell the farm and move back here? We have enough land to build you and the children a house."

Mama faced Clara. "Or you can find a nice man here who already owns a farm."

"I agree," Alfred said. "A man who's willing to be a father to John and Edna too."

If Clara didn't know any better, it sounded like Papa, Mama, and Alfred already had a man in mind.

Susan shook her head. "Abram is in Virginia. Asking her to leave him is disrespectful."

About to eat a bite of mashed potatoes, Edna lowered the fork. "What do they mean, Mama? I don't want to leave Papa. I like sitting by his cross and talking to him."

Clara pulled Edna close and told her not to worry. Despite how Amish and Mennonite men were supposed to rule their households, Clara would not be bullied into taking her children far away from their Papa, regardless of whether he was alive or not. To them he was alive, and if that gave them peace, no one would take that peace away. Sitting up straight, she held her shoulders back and faced the three members of her family who were determined to rule her life. "I'm a grown woman. I have a family and I run my own farm. The person who thinks they can force me to leave it better think again."

Susan winked at her. Beside her, Daniel winked at Clara too. Mama went back to eating. Alfred pursed his lips, his familiar habit of disapproval. Papa cleared his throat. "We're just trying to help, Clara."

"Make them stop, Mama," Edna said. "Call Jonah and let's go home. I don't like it here."

Blinking tears, John shook a finger at Papa. "You're a bad, bad man. You made Edna cry."

Clara pulled her precious children close. "Shh, it's all right. We'll never leave our home and your papa."

Susan stood. Her freckled cheeks flared scarlet.

"Beachy Amish Mennonite or not, men ruling the house or not, this is *no* way to treat family. They lost the most important man in the world to them barely six months ago, and you hound them the first time they visit us?" She threw her napkin down. "It makes me want to move to Virginia myself."

Daniel stood to place an arm around her shoulders. "The children will be home from school soon, let's go." At the door, after donning a coat and a wide-brimmed black hat, he thanked Mama for the meal. Taking her coat from a hanger, Susan left without a word, leaving Daniel to catch the screened door before it slammed behind her.

Edna stopped crying. Clara tried to get her to eat a little more, but she refused. John just glared at Papa, whose mouth gaped.

Blinking back tears, Mama looked at him. "I think we need to apologize." She wiped her eyes and faced Clara. "Do you remember Noah Miller? You were in the same class together. You were good friends until you met Abram."

Clara remembered Noah. She had hoped he would ask Papa to court her when they got old enough. What a smile he had, and he was as kind and gentle as Abram had been. His green eyes and blond hair were remarkable as well. The last she had heard of him, he was courting a woman from another community a few miles away. Susan said he hadn't courted anyone before that woman because she thought Clara marrying Abram had broken his heart. Guessing he hadn't married that woman, Clara faced Mama. "Yes, I remember him. Do I have to ask why you want to know?"

"We're your family," Alfred said. "Is it wrong for us to be concerned about you and the children in Virginia alone?"

John took a handful of mashed potatoes from his plate and drew them back over his shoulder. Before he could throw them at Alfred, Clara grabbed his arm and cleaned his hand with a napkin. "That's enough. I said we're not leaving our home and that's final. You and Edna go sit on the sofa." After they did, Clara moved to the chair across from Mama. Beside Alfred, Rebecca kept her head down. Clara loved God and all of His teachings. Although the Bible had many verses about submitting to a husband, it also said husbands should honor their wives, going on to say she is an equal partner in God's gift of new life. This was how she and Abram lived, honoring each other in all things, including household decisions and decisions about the children. The result had been the blessing of more happiness than she could imagine, and she refused to settle for less, regardless of the man.

"See there," Papa said. "Without a man in the home, John has no discipline."

Anger flooded Clara in wave after wave. She stood. "My children had plenty of discipline until you pushed them too far." She took her phone from her dress pocket. "I can call Jonah right now and go home, or you can apologize."

Papa glared at Mama. "This is what we get by letting her marry Abram and move away—an ungrateful daughter."

Mama held out her hand toward Clara. "Please pass the mashed potatoes." She took them when Clara offered them, then held the bowl toward Papa. "In all the years I've known Clara, she has always been grateful. You can apologize now, or I'll finish what my grandson started."

Again, Papa's mouth gaped. "You wouldn't dare."

"Yes, I'd dare, just like I did when you tried to kiss me the first time you walked me home from Sunday singing. If you remember correctly, I was carrying a leftover bowl of mashed potatoes from lunch that day."

Papa's lips tightened. His eyes bulged. Then he sputtered into a huge laugh, even slapping his knee. Done with his laugh, he kissed Mama's cheek. "It isn't my fault you were the prettiest girl in the community back then."

Mama dipped a finger in the mashed potatoes and dotted the tip of his nose with them. "What do you mean 'back then?' Aren't I now?"

Nodding, he faced Clara. "I'll be on my knees tonight to beg God for forgiveness. I have no excuse for offending you, except to say I worry about you and the children. You would feel the same if they were far away and weren't sure how they were."

Glad the crisis had passed, Clara accepted his apology. "Now that we've come to an understanding," she added, "what's this about Noah Miller?"

"He never married the woman he was courting," Alfred said. "When we told him about Abram, he almost cried from worry about you and the children."

Clara started to say she'd like to see him, but she remembered how she had planned to tell Papa about Vernon. If Noah were the same sweet man she knew from long ago, she was afraid her decision about Vernon might come back to trouble her. Still, she couldn't go back on her word unless something happened to make her change her mind.

She went to kiss Papa's cheek and accept his apology again. Mama rose to hug her and apologized too. She and Papa called John and Edna over to tell them how much they loved them and how sorry they were for upsetting them. They accepted graciously, like Clara knew they would. Alfred and Rebecca said their goodbyes, saying they would be back before Clara left. Papa took John and Edna outside for a walk around the farm. As Clara helped Mama clear the table and wash the dishes, Mama told her how Noah lived on the farm bordering their farm to the back, plus how his home was only a short walk through the woods. She didn't say anything else, nor did she need to. The implication was clear: if Clara visited Noah, they might marry, which would allow her and the children to live close by.

Clara dried a dish and put it away. "You say his house is just a short walk through the woods?"

"That's right," Mama said, giving her another dish. "Just a short walk away. He's even more handsome than when you were teenagers."

The decision to see Noah or tell her parents about Vernon teetered back and forth in Clara's mind as if she were in the center of a seesaw as a child.

She shrugged.

There was nothing wrong with doing both, and that's exactly what she would do when the dishes were done.

Chapter 12

Entering the path in the woods, Clara breathed in the tangy scent of oak, maple, and hickory leaves overhead. The trees formed an amazing tunnel of color surrounding her. Although she loved spring, with its greening and budding plants, she loved the fall almost as much, with its cool mornings, brisk air, and red, gold, and orange leaves.

Behind her, at a fence she had just passed, Papa was showing John and Edna the last milk cow he had bought, saying he hadn't named her yet. The children started suggesting names. "Bossy?" Edna asked.

John giggled. "That's *your* name," which prompted a chuckle from Papa.

Clara silently thanked God for intervening in the earlier argument with Papa, including Mama's part in turning a serious moment into a humorous one by mentioning their past concerning mashed potatoes.

Still, Clara had no doubts about Mama wanting her to move nearby, even if it took marrying Noah to do so. When she had told her how she was going to visit him after washing the dishes, her crinkling eyes had revealed her happiness at the idea. Regardless, Clara had no intention of moving back to Pennsylvania. Her life was in Virginia now, and her family here needed to accept that.

In the path, recently fallen leaves crunched underfoot. A gray squirrel raced up a tree with a hickory nut in its mouth. Its fluffy tail streamed behind it as it disappeared into the yellow leaves. At the end of the path about fifty steps ahead, a small house loomed in the distance. No trees surrounded the single-story home. Instead of a tin roof, dark shingles covered it. A tractor sat beneath a shed built onto the side of a barn. A pickup truck sat in the gravel driveway. Gray vinyl siding covered the house instead of white-painted planks, like some Mennonites in the area used to cover their homes. To one side of the house, holding a basket and wearing wide-brimmed straw hat to ward of the sun, Noah pulled a bell pepper and placed it in the basket.

At the sight of him, memories of their walks after

Sunday singing flooded Clara, especially the one time he had dared to hold her hand. At fifteen, he had been average in size and height. Now, at twenty-five like Clara, he was broad shouldered like Abram, but not quite as tall. He removed his hat and wiped sweat from his forehead with the back of his hand. Unlike some of the Old Order Amish men, with their haircuts shaped as if a wife or a mother had placed a bowl over their heads as a trimming guide, Noah's blond curls were trimmed short on top of his head and tapered at the nape of his neck. Not having married yet, he wore no beard either. Even so, beard length in Beachy Amish Mennonite communities varied. In Clara's community, for example, some married men preferred shorter beards. Although Vernon's wife had died, he still wore a short beard. Even though the news of her death had countered the rumor of their divorce, the situation of how that rumor had begun to start with made no sense to Clara.

She left the path. Facing away from her, Noah picked another pepper. Clara snuck up behind him. "Look at you, out in your garden picking peppers. You'll make some man a fine wife one day."

Noah turned, and he dropped the basket of peppers. "Clara? Is it really you?"

Despite not seeing him for years, Clara gave him

a quick hug. "Of course it's me. Who else would tease you like I used to?"

He beamed a huge smile. "You haven't changed a bit." His smile faded. "I can't tell you how sorry I was to hear about Abram. I would've come to the funeral, but I was going through a difficult time myself."

Clara wondered if he meant when he stopped courting the woman he had been seeing. Mama hadn't mentioned a timeline, so that might be the case. Another question shocked Clara. Could Noah have stopped courting the woman when he heard about Abram's death? If so, that might mean he hoped they could pick up the pieces of their past and start over again.

Noah picked up the basket. "Won't you come inside and have some tea? It won't take a minute, and I'd love to catch up."

Clara studied the horizon, darkening to night. "I can't stay long. The children and I are visiting for a few days. I haven't unpacked yet."

Noah quirked his mouth to one side with his familiar lop-sided grin. "You just want me to walk you home in the dark." He took her by the hand. "Come on, just one cup of tea and a short talk. Then I'll let you go."

As he tugged her along, the feelings she had experienced as a fifteen-year-old girl returned —

feelings of warmth and attraction, of admiration and wonder, of the curiosity of what it would feel like to kiss—

Jonah?

Why had his name popped into her mind when she was holding Noah's hand? She had vowed to never think of him in such a way again, and she was doing it yet again.

On the porch, Noah released her hand to open the door. He followed her inside and set the basket on a table about half the size of hers at home. Its grain suggested oak. The wooden pegs suggested it was hand-made. Clara recalled how Noah had started wood working the year she left. She went to a rocking chair by the fireplace and ran her fingertips along the armrest. "This is beautiful work, Noah."

Filling a teapot with water at the sink, he faced her. "Well, I like to stay busy. It keeps my mind occupied."

She joined him at the sink. His shirt smelled of fresh air and sunshine, like Abram's did after a day outside.

Noah went to the propane stove and set the teapot on a burner. He suggested they wait in the two rocking chairs by the fireplace. Clara noted many more pieces of handmade furniture around the combination living room and kitchen: a thick slab of oak for the mantle over the fireplace, corner tables, a dish cabinet, a bookcase that reached to the ceiling, a coat rack by the door, a set of wooden hangers on the wall, one of which held Noah's hat.

"What do you think of my home?" he asked, drawing her attention back to him.

"If you've been this busy making furniture since I left, is the rest of the house filled with it?"

"It is," Noah said, his voice soft and sweet. "And with memories of ..." His intense green eyes finished his sentence: *Of you.*

Clara's cheeks flared heat. Maybe his memories were of the woman he had courted and not of her. She swallowed, hoping to settle the emotions roiling in her chest. "Do you mind if I ask about the woman you were courting? Mama told me."

Noah's mouth opened and closed. "You would hate me like her parents do." He leaned forward to set his elbows on his knees and clasp his hands together. "I didn't think we were a good match. When I told her, it broke her heart. I didn't know she cared so much. I know how that feels, and I didn't feel it for her. That's why I didn't think we were a good match."

The water in the teapot gurgled to a boil. In the window to the left, the coming night darkened the curtain. Somewhere in the woods, a whippoorwill called, *whip-poor-will, whip-poor-will, whip-poor-will.* Then its call faded, lost in Clara's memories of her walks with Noah and the single time they had held hands, fireflies flickering their yellow tails on a lingering summer evening.

She couldn't recall why she had chosen Abram over Noah. Maybe it was for the same reason Noah hadn't chosen the girl, because he hadn't fallen in love with her like he had with Clara. Not only that, he still loved her. The realization that a man could feel so strongly for her after she had married and moved away and had children amazed her. Might they have a second chance now, and if so, would Abram approve? After all, regardless of any shame she might feel for rejecting Vernon, she desired love in her second marriage as much as she had in the first.

The teapot whistled. Noah made tea, asking Clara if she liked honey and lemon in it like she used to. His lingering memory of such a simple thing astounded her. She went to him and waited while he finished stirring. His broad shoulders, his blond hair, and his tender heart all combined to make her want to slip her hands around his waist and hold him tight. Instead, she took the offered cup and returned to the rocking chair.

No, the desire to hold him came from missing

how she used to hold Abram that way. She needed to get her mind back on her promise to court Vernon and to stop thinking of those things that attracted her to Noah.

After sitting, Noah sipped tea. He didn't look at her, although she expected him to. She sipped as well, enjoying the honey and lemon. It occurred to her how she hadn't put honey and lemon in her tea after she married Abram. Maybe it was a memory of her and Noah's time together that she had decided to hold as a keepsake of her youth.

Noah sipped again. "It's good to see you. Did you name your children John and Edna like we talked about?"

Puzzled, Clara swallowed the tea she was sipping. "I don't remember talking to you about naming my children."

"We talked about naming *our* children. I suppose you've forgotten." Noah's voice carried more than a hint of sadness. Still, Clara knew they hadn't talked about naming children, no matter who the father was.

He tapped his fingertips on the cup. "I've been thinking about buying a bigger farm. My father has offered to help. He says it might do me good to get away after I ended the courtship. Do you know of any land available in Virginia?"

No doubt, Clara knew, to be close to her so they

could rekindle their relationship. She was a weak, willful woman, only thinking about herself, which Amish and Mennonites weren't supposed to do. It was time to put an end to any idea of being with him. "I'm sorry about your courtship," she said, meaning it. "If you ended it because of what happened to Abram, you shouldn't have. I don't intend to court anyone—much less marry—anytime soon."

Noah grinned his lopsided grin. "You think I ended my courtship because I wanted you back after what happened to Abram. You do realize we aren't supposed to be prideful."

Clara was tempted to throw the tea in his face. She took the cup to the table. "I thought it would be good to see you and it was, but it didn't take long to get my fill of you."

As she opened the door, Noah hurried over. "Your tone says you don't want me to walk you through the woods." He opened a cabinet for a flashlight and offered it to her. "I'm sorry if I upset you, but I wouldn't be able to do that if you didn't still care about me. See you soon."

Clara snatched the flashlight and hurried toward the path. She turned it on as the dark tunnel formed by the overhanging trees closed around her to block any hint of starlight. Maybe she had chosen Abram because of Noah's arrogance. If so, she had made the right choice.

Chapter 13

Clara entered the back door of her parent's home, which opened to a mud room where Papa kept his work boots and coat. Intending to return the flashlight to Noah tomorrow, she left it on a shelf and opened the door to the inside of the house. This door led to a hall that led to the kitchen and family room. Halfway along the darkened hall, she stopped. In the living area, Mama and Papa were talking to someone. Then that someone answered, and that someone was Vernon.

She peeked into her room. Edna and John were in two cots by her bed. Clara didn't know what to think about Vernon coming here. She had told him she would ask Papa about courting him, and that's how she wanted to handle it. At least the children wouldn't hear any possible arguments.

She took a single step and stopped. Abram had

often admired her spirit, but he said she sometimes allowed her emotion to overrule her commitment to their Ordnung's way of doing what was best for the family and the community, choosing instead what she thought was best for herself. This particular doctrine confused Clara more than any other. If the members of a community lived in such a way as to honor God, especially when choosing love in marriage instead of the mere notion of marrying to strengthen a community with family ties, wouldn't love be the better choice to strengthen a community? She had asked Abram this question more than once. He said he understood because of how they had married for love, but he also said many couples grew to love each other regardless. She knew this to be true as well; Alison's marriage was an example. Still, if she had to marry to strengthen her community, she could choose worse than Vernon. If they did marry, maybe their love would grow in time. First, though, he needed to know how she didn't appreciate him coming up here behind her back. Amish and Mennonites valued honesty, and his doing so was dishonest.

When she entered the room, Mama, Papa, and Vernon were sitting at the table with coffee. Vernon held up a sandwich. "Ah, there you are. Did you have a nice visit with Noah? It's good to see old friends, isn't it?"

"Like I've been telling you," Papa said, "she and Noah are more than old friends."

"*Much* more," Mama said.

Vernon patted the chair beside him. "Come sit while I finish my sandwich. Then we can share our news."

Mama and Papa said nothing. They likely had guessed Vernon's news but were hoping Clara had news of her visit with Noah. She, however, wanted to speak with Vernon alone first, or there wouldn't be any news to tell. She told him to finish his sandwich because she needed to talk to him outside about something. To make her request clearer, she poured coffee and waited by the door, ignoring him when he asked her to sit again.

Mama and Papa's eyes widened as they looked at each other. They knew Clara's headstrong streak as well as Abram had. Vernon finished the sandwich and coffee and opened the door. Sipping her own coffee, Clara ignored him. If they were going to court, he should get a good dose of her headstrong streak like everyone else in her family had.

As they stood there, their wills in a battle against each other, Clara thought of Jonah. He certainly knew her headstrong streak, and he seemed to actually enjoy it. She couldn't even say that about Abram, although she *could* say it about Noah. She finished the coffee and took the cup to the sink. Without a word, she turned the front porch light on and went outside, expecting Vernon to follow if he wanted to court her. Guiding her by her elbow, he led her away from the screened door. She went back to close the wooden door. If he wanted privacy, so did she, and it was best to discuss matters like theirs in private.

As they stood facing each other, Clara could feel her anger rising. How dare Vernon come here without telling her. They had decided she would tell her parents and here he was, running after her like he didn't trust her.

He ran his fingers through his brown hair. "I'm sure you're upset. Does it matter that I missed you to the point of driving straight here with only one stop? When I mentioned it, your mother even made me a sandwich." He took Clara's hands in his. "Please forgive me. I know we agreed you would ask your father about us courting, but I did miss you."

Clara noted how he hadn't mentioned John and Edna.

"How are John and Edna?" he asked. "Did they enjoy the drive with Jonah? I saw him at the hotel in Buck when I got a room. He really is a fine friend to you and the children."

Vernon's concern drained the anger from Clara. She had never seen him this way, clutching her hands, his voice tender, even quavering with emotion. She led him to two rocking chairs. "I'm not angry. I just don't like it when someone tells me they'll do something and they don't."

Vernon hung his head. "I know, and I'm sorry." His hands shook in his lap. The drive here was ... I don't have the words for it. I got lost several times, even with a GPS. The traffic around Washington, D.C. was terrible. I prayed so much, I ran out of things to pray."

Imagining Vernon on the verge of a nervous breakdown in the middle of traffic, all while the GPS said in its monotone voice to make a U-turn over and over again, made Clara giggle. "Well," she said, trying to get it under control, "maybe you'll have to hire Jonah to drive you on a long trip instead of using a GPS."

Vernon chuckled. "That's not a bad idea. I've always wanted to see the ocean. I'd rather ride than drive any day." He snapped his fingers. "After we tell you parents about our plans to court when you're ready, we can ask Jonah to take us to Corolla, on the Outer Banks of North Carolina. I've always wanted to see the wild horses there. I'm sure John and Edna would love it. I'd pay all the expenses, of course."

Although Clara appreciated Vernon's offer, she wasn't ready to court him yet. Too many memories of Abram lingered around their home and in her heart. Yes, she needed to move on eventually, but now was too soon.

Vernon tilted his head to one side. "You're not saying anything. Is something wrong?"

"I know I need to move on from Abram's death eventually, but now is too soon. We can ask Mama and Papa about courting, but it may be a while before I'm ready." Clara paused, unsure what Vernon would think of her next statement. "Please don't take this the wrong way," she said, touching his sleeve, "but my courting you doesn't mean I'll marry you. It's to get to know each other first. I won't marry until we know we'll be a good match. Do you understand?"

Vernon again took her hands in his. "That's one of the things I admire about you—you think things through instead of making rash decisions. Of course I understand." He stood from the rocking chair. "Can we ask your parents now, or would you like to wait until tomorrow? Then they'll have all day to get used to the idea before they decide."

"You were reading my mind," Clara said, smiling at him. "Let's wait until tomorrow."

"I'll tell them goodnight." Vernon yawned. "I'm ready to get back to town and go to sleep."

Clara followed Vernon inside. He thanked Mama and Papa for their hospitality and said he'd be back tomorrow. When he left, Mama and Papa eyed Clara. "Your bishop seems like a nice man," Papa said. "Why did he drive all the way here to see you when he could've called?"

"I agree," Mama said, worry in her voice—a worry, no doubt, that Vernon might ruin her plans for Clara and Noah to marry and live nearby.

Clara didn't know how to answer their questions. She didn't want to lie, but she didn't want to tell the truth either. "You'll just have to wait and see until tomorrow, won't you? Goodnight."

In her room, which had an adjoining bathroom, she kissed her fingertips and touched them to John and Edna's cheeks. Wearing a simple nightgown, she went to the bathroom to brush her teeth and unpin her hair. Then she washed her face and sat on the side of the bed to braid her hair to avoid tangles while she slept. About to turn off the lamp, she grabbed her ringing phone and checked the screen. Expecting Vernon, she raised her eyebrows at Jonah's number. She whispered "hello" to him and asked why he was calling.

"Are you in bed?" he asked.

"Just now," she said. "I have to whisper because John and Edna are in here."

"I saw Vernon checking into the hotel. He said he was going to surprise you. How did it go?"

For some reason Clara couldn't explain, she didn't want to talk about Vernon. "What did you have for supper?"

"Just a burger and fries at a fast-food place. Did you and Vernon ask your parents about courting?"

"Tomorrow."

"That's it? Just 'tomorrow?'"

Clara rolled over and ran her hand over the other pillow. Despite vowing not to think of Jonah that way again, she imagined him lying there, facing her.

"Clara?"

"Hmm?"

"Is something wrong?"

"I ..."

"What?"

"I miss you. You know, as friends."

"I miss you too."

"I wish ..."

"What?"

Clara knew better than to suggest it, but she needed to get out of the house. "I wish we could take a ride in the country. I want to roll the windows down and smell the night air and park and listen to the crickets chirp and to the whip—"

"To the whippoorwills, right?"

"Yes. I love how they sound lonely but not, because they're calling to each other." Clara couldn't say the rest: *like we're lonely and talking to each other.*

"If you really want to, I can be there in ten minutes. I wouldn't mind getting out of my room myself and enjoying the night air."

Clara closed her eyes. Not only was she being selfish, it went against everything she believed as a Beachy Amish woman. Like she had told herself time and time again, her purpose was to honor God through commitment to her family and to her community, and to avoid all thoughts of self. Tears filled her eyes. She loved God and his teachings, but to ignore her feelings might cause her to swell and explode like a child's overinflated balloon. If that happened, there was no telling what she might do, like telling Jonah she loved him and to take her away from here to a life where she could tend to her own feelings, at least part of the time instead of none of the time.

She told Jonah she would meet him down the road to keep his truck from waking anyone and ended the call. Wearing a blue dress and leaving her hair braided, she put on tennis shoes, a light jacket for the September air, ignored the kapp on the dresser, and hurried out the back door.

Standing beneath a huge oak tree, she enjoyed the rattle of its leaves from the occasional breeze. Clara shivered in the cold. Frost sparkled on the grass, illuminated by moonlight. The night air chilled her sinuses. Her breath formed little white puffs before her face.

A pair of headlights appeared down the road. The rumble of a diesel engine followed. Jonah stopped. She climbed in the truck, and he continued down the road, saying nothing. A few miles later they went over a bridge spanning a creek. On the other side of the bridge, Jonah steered into a dirt road that went down to the bank, possibly made by people fishing. Within a grove of maple trees, their leaves scarlet in the headlights, he killed the engine and looked at Clara. "I like your braid. As long as it is, you could lasso your milk cow with it."

Clara started to laugh. Then she covered her face and cried. "I shouldn't be here," she sobbed. "I'm Beachy Amish Mennonite and I shouldn't be here."

Jonah gently pulled her hands from her face. "I shouldn't be here either but I am. You're one of the strongest women I know, but what you're going through is terrible. You lost your husband. You're trying to raise your children alone. You're thinking about courting Vernon when you don't love him. Your parents probably want you to move back here and marry someone else. And that's just the things I can guess."

Clara couldn't see Jonah's face in the darkness, but she knew he was only inches away. She placed his hands on the truck's console and lay her head on them. "How do you know so much about me, Jonah?"

He eased one hand free and stroked her hair. "That's not important. What's important is what you know about yourself. I can't figure out your life for you. Only you can do that."

"It's so hard. When Abram was alive, I was happier than I ever thought possible. Now I question everything. As much as I hate to say it, I even question being Beachy Amish Mennonite. Just being here with you is supposed to be a disgrace. If someone saw us, especially with my hair down, they would think terrible things about me."

Clara sat up. With her eyes adjusted to the dark, she could see the outline of Jonah's face. "I miss Abram so much. He was my best friend, but you're my best friend now. Is it wrong to ask my best friend to hold me?"

Jonah raised the steering wheel and moved the

seat back. Clara climbed into his lap. He wrapped his arms around her and pulled her close. She rested her head on his shoulder. "Abram used to hold me like this. I miss him so much."

Although the air inside the truck soon cooled, they grew warm from their combined body heat. Clara yawned. "What time is it?"

Jonah pushed a button on his watch, which illuminated its dial. "10:15. Are you ready to go?"

Clara answered by snuggling into his warmth. "You make me feel safe, Jonah, like being with you would solve all my problems."

With the tip of her braid, he tickled her nose. "Hey, that's what best friends are for."

Clara wondered if God would forgive her this transgression. She prayed that He would, that He understood all her fears and questions, that He didn't mind Jonah holding her in the night with her hair down and her kapp off.

Jonah lowered his window, evidenced by the crisp and cool night air coming in. Mixed with the gurgling of the creek, two whippoorwills called to each other. To Clara, one sound was soothing. The other one, though, was the lonely call of two hearts, perhaps of even her heart and Jonah's heart beating as two instead of one, never to be joined as anything but friends.

He turned the truck key, which illuminated the

dashboard lights. "I've been studying the Beachy Amish Mennonites online. I know they don't allow radios in the home or musical instruments in church, and I don't understand it. The Bible says to praise God with musical instruments, so how can it be wrong?"

Clara said nothing. With all the questions she had been asking herself lately, who was she to judge?

Jonah turned the radio on. "This is bluegrass gospel music. The bands usually have a guitar, a banjo, a fiddle, and a bass. Sometimes they have a mandolin and a dobro too." He changed channels. "All right, this is my favorite song. It's called *In the Sweet Bye and Bye.*"

The music and words filled Clara's soul. Never had she heard anything so beautiful. More voices joined the first voice, and they blended in a mesmerizing mix that made tears come to her eyes.

"It's a song about meeting again after we die," Jonah said, "like you'll meet Abram again after you die. I love the line about meeting on that beautiful shore."

"It *is* beautiful," Clara said.

Jonah turned the radio off. "It is, but I don't want to make you question your faith. I just thought you'd like to hear what you've been missing." He laughed. "Now if I were a Beachy Amish bishop, and my congregation agreed, I might shake things up a bit."

Feeling much better from Jonah holding her, plus from hearing the music she had never heard before, Clara moved back to the other seat. "Oh, the Beachy Amish Mennonites are quite different from the Old Order Amish."

"I agree," Jonah said, amusement in his voice. "As you might know, the only technology the Swartzentruber Amish allow is a washing machine operated by a generator."

Clara giggled. "Of course it is. No woman wants to wash clothes for a family of six or eight or ten or more. She wouldn't have time to cook all those meals either, and you men just *have* to have your food on time."

Jonah tapped the LED clock on the radio. "It's almost eleven, I better get you home." As he started to turn the key, Clara leaned over the console to hug his neck. He returned the hug. When she was in her seat again, he cupped her cheek in his palm. "Do you have any idea how special you are, Clara? Vernon is a blessed man, but I'm blessed to be your neighbor. Anytime you need me, day or night, just call and I'll come running."

The warmth of Jonah's palm, as well as his sincere words, melted Clara's heart. "I'm blessed to be your neighbor too, Jonah. You're so good to me and the children. I don't know what we'd do without you."

Jonah cranked the truck. "I think God brought us together for a reason. Right now I think that reason is to get you home."

When the truck left the maple grove, millions upon millions of stars sparkled in the night sky over the road. To Clara, each could be an ancestor looking down on her to see what life held for her, plus what choices she would make to affect her life.

Jonah dropped her off. As she stood in the open truck door, they shared a smile. Then he left, and she sank to her knees in tears. She wasn't in control of her life; it was in control of her. Rule after rule forced her to follow more rules she didn't understand, like rules about musical instruments and who she could or couldn't love.

Wiping tears, she walked to the house. The frost glistened on the grass in the moonlight. Like before, her breaths made little puffs of white. The crisp air, colder now, burned her sinuses and throat.

In bed again, she cuddled her pillow while pulling the other pillow close like she had pulled Jonah close.

It had been wrong to go out with him and park beneath the stars. She shoved the pillow away.

Tomorrow was a new day—a new day for her and Vernon to ask Mama and Papa about courting each other.

Despite her conviction, she pulled the pillow close again. Even if she came to care about Vernon enough to marry him, she would always have her best friend close by.

Clara closed her eyes. *Dear God, please forgive me for being a weak woman. You know I think more of Jonah than a friend, but is it wrong to do that? Like with how You gave us your Son because You love us despite our sins, isn't love your most precious gift to both man and woman regardless of our religion?*

From the teachings in the Bible, Clara knew the answer. She rolled over to see John and Edna sleeping in their cots, both lit by the soft glow of moonlight streaming through the window. Her children were her focus, not her. They needed a father, and Vernon was willing to take that role in their lives.

Clara closed her eyes again. *Thank you for showing me the way, Lord. Thy will be done, amen.*

Out in the night, two whippoorwills called to each other, confusing Clara yet again as to God's will for her and the children.

She pressed her palm to her cheek. Jonah's touch had comforted her beyond measure, yet they would never be together. If she and Vernon didn't marry, the embers of her and Noah's past were waiting to be fanned into flame again.

As this thought left Clara's mind, more thoughts entered it: Although it seemed Jonah and Lydia were siblings, something about it felt off. And why did her elbow appear to have been broken and surgically repaired? And who had bought the propane stove? And did Vernon's wife really die as he had said, or was the rumor about his wife divorcing him true?

No answers presented themselves, so Clara decided to get some sleep. After all, she and Vernon would likely get permission to court from Mama and Papa tomorrow, and she needed to tell Abram's parents after, as well as letting them visit with the children. Then she would have to decide how long her mourning period would last. So many things would change when that happened, one being her and Vernon going to Corolla to see the wild horses he had mentioned. Yes, it would be a good way to get to know each other, and if Jonah agreed to take them, she would have her best friend nearby to comfort her if the need arose.

Like a warm bath in winter, sleep washed over Clara. Dreams of Abram holding her filled the night, followed by Vernon's kindness, followed by Noah's smiling green eyes, followed by Jonah holding her as the call of whippoorwills echoed in the night.

Yes, her heart was calling for love, but in the end, who would that love be?

Follow your heart, Abram's sweet voice said, waking her to tears. *Like the love we shared for too short a time, find it again. Only a life filled with a love like ours will truly make us happy.*

Clara didn't understand what he meant by a love like "ours" when he was gone.

I'm not gone, Clara. You know I'm always with you, deep in your heart. All I pray for is your happiness. Now sleep and be strong. Do what you know is right, and it all will work out.

Clara drifted off again, secure in her decision to do the right thing.

But one question remained:

What about love?

Readers: please enjoy the first chapter of the second book in the Clara Engelman Series, *Clara's Courtship,* due to be published later this year.

Beside Clara in Abram's old pickup truck, Alison pointed at one of the pedals in the floor. "No, Clara. The one on the left is the clutch, not the brake. You let out on that one and push the accelerator at the same time."

Clara tried again, causing the truck to buck and bounce until it stalled. On the porch to her right, Edna and John cackled with laughter. Clara stuck her head out the truck window. "If I remember correctly, and I do, a certain young lady has her sixth birthday soon. If she wants pizza, she better stop cackling at her mama like a hen laying an egg."

"That's all right," Edna said, her cheeks red from laughing. "John's birthday is next month. We can have pizza then."

John smiled at Edna. "That's right, Edna. And Jonah can make strawberry ice cream."

Clara loved her children beyond measure. They were growing so fast. Not only would Edna be six soon, John would be five next month."

She pressed the clutch down and cranked the truck. After a deep breath, she eased out on the clutch and pressed the accelerator at the same time. The truck moved forward as it should, unlike a bucking horse.

"Good job," Alison said. "You do fine on the road. If we can get you started without jarring my teeth out, you can get your license soon. Now try it in reverse."

Clara did so, glad she was improving. Edna would start school in her community in Nathalie on the first of September, and Clara needed to drive her there by 8:30 every morning.

She stopped the truck and backed it past the porch, where Edna and John clapped wildly. Clara took one hand off the steering wheel to wave, which made the truck swerve to the left. Alison grabbed the wheel. "Clara! Pay attention!"

Clara grabbed the wheel with both hands, happy she hadn't hit Alison's pickup parked to one side of the driveway. "I'm sorry. What do the English say about race car driving? I almost did that."

"'Swapping paint.' Don't you dare. Samuel just bought our truck. He wouldn't like a blue streak on the white paint."

Clara went forward and backward a few more times. "I think I've got the hang of the clutch now." She parked beside Alison's truck. As she started to get out, Alison grabbed her arm.

"Whoa there. Tell me when you plan to stop mourning and court Vernon. You've made him wait almost a year."

When Clara had called Alison to come for another driving lesson, she had expected this question to come up. Although her thoughts of Abram were more positive after more than a year without him, she sometimes broke down in tears late at night, when she woke from reaching for him in the bed and only found the empty place where he used to sleep.

Alison shoved her shoulder. "Stop ignoring me and answer my question. Oh, *I* know what it is," she said, waggling her finger at Clara. "You've got too many men to choose from—a handsome neighbor right next door and an old flame back in Pennsylvania along with Vernon. How's Noah anyway? Has he called lately?"

"Yes, Miss Nosy," Clara said, uselessly trying to shame her best friend. "For an Amish woman, you like to ask personal questions."

"I ask because you won't tell me anything otherwise. Is Noah still thinking about buying some land around here? You know it's just to be near you. Maybe you could court Vernon a few months and court Noah a few months and decide who you want."

Ignoring Alison, Clara got out of the truck. Both Vernon and Noah were Beachy Amish Mennonite like her, but she didn't have the same feelings for them as she had for her neighbor, Jonah.

Unfortunately, he wasn't any kind of Amish, so she had to constantly tell herself to stop thinking about him as a possible husband. Regardless though, she did think about him as a possible husband. Not only did he understand her struggle with the decision to court Vernon when she didn't love him, he had been helping her with the farm ever since they met, more than a year ago. He had also saved Edna's life by taking her to the hospital in South Boston, when a Black Widow spider bit her. To Clara's astonishment, when a nurse had taken her to see Edna in intensive care for the first time, Jonah pretended to be her husband so he could go too, and he had cried at seeing Edna lying in the bed with a ventilator tube filling her small chest with air. Of the three men in her life, it was a shame how Clara couldn't court Jonah. They were as alike as her and Abram had been. She could count on him like she could count on God sending the rain in the spring to help the flowers bloom and her garden to grow.

On the way to the porch and the waiting children, Clara pulled Alison aside. "Stop your teasing about Jonah. I don't want John and Edna to get the wrong idea."

"Wrong idea?" Alison sputtered. "You're the one with the wrong idea and you know it. Why don't you tell him how you feel? He might become

Amish so you two can be together."

"You have lost your mind," Clara said, leaving Alison.

On the porch, John and Edna clapped again. "When can we go to town?" Edna asked.

"Me too," John said. "I wanna pick my birthday present."

Clara climbed the steps and tousled his hair. "No, sir. It's a surprise. Besides, I explained how we give simple gifts and not extravagant ones because we're Amish."

"What's 'stravagant?" John asked. "I just want a toy boat."

"Me too," Edna said. "We can play with them in the lake when Jonah takes us fishing again."

"My, my," Alison said from the bottom of the steps. "It must be nice to have someone like Jonah to take you fishing on the lake." She faced Clara. "Let me know when you want to take your driver test and I'll take you." She winked. "Unless Jonah can take you." She waved at John and Edna. "Make your mama behave, you two. See you later."

Edna tugged Clara's dress. "Why did she make that face at you, Mama? Did she have something in her eye?"

"That's called a wink," Clara said. "People do that when they say silly things." She opened the door. "It's late and I need to cook supper. Both of you wash up so you can help."

"No, Mama," Edna said, stamping her foot on the porch's wooden boards. "We haven't talked to Papa today."

Shame warmed Clara's cheeks. Without fail, unless weather intervened, she and the children had visited Abram's grave behind the house, beneath the huge limbs of an old oak tree. She apologized to Edna and told her and John to come along.

The sun shone brightly on them until they entered the shade. Edna went straight to the single white cross made of painted wood and touched it. "We're here, Papa." She looked up and waved. "I hope you're having a good day."

Having never seen Edna do this, John looked up too. "Is Papa in the tree? I thought he's in Heaven."

"He is," Clara said. "Edna's just waving to him through the tree."

John waved too. "Hi, Papa." He went to the cross and touched it, then faced Clara. "Will we ever have another papa? I want one to take us fishing like Jonah did that time."

"Me too," Edna said.

Clara said nothing. At least they hadn't mentioned having Jonah for a papa. As much as they enjoyed being with him, and he with them, it was a wonder.

Clara touched the cross and stepped back while the children told Abram about their day, plus their coming birthdays. They didn't say so, but she knew they wished he were here like she wished he were here.

It was hard to believe over a year had passed since his death. So much had happened since then too, including her miscarriage on the same day the spider had bitten Edna.

Although her family's community was over thirty minutes away by vehicle, they had taken up an offering to help her after Abram died. As grateful as Clara was for them, if the truth be told, she was more grateful for Jonah. Even with the puzzle of who Lydia was, the woman who lived with him, he and Clara had grown close over the past year. He had even driven her and the children to Pennsylvania last year around this time so they could visit Clara's and Abram's parents. During the visit, she had planned to ask her parent's permission to court Vernon when she felt like her mourning period was over. Then he had come there without telling her, right when she had come home from visiting Noah, who she had wanted to court when she was fifteen. That night, Jonah had called from his hotel room to see how she was. Knowing it was wrong, she had suggested they go for a drive. She had even left her hair down. They had parked near a creek, where she had broken down in tears. Typical for Jonah, with how he seemed to know her so well, he had told her she would have to make her own choices in life. Regardless, she had asked him to comfort her by holding her, but as best friends only. She had done so by crawling into his lap like a child, and he had held her like a child. Except for when Abram had held her, she had never felt so safe. What a blessing Jonah was. If only, like Alison had teased, he was Amish, Clara would court him in a heartbeat. Then again, the question of his and Lydia's true relationship stayed stuck in the back of Clara's mind as if it were a tick stuck to a dog.

The children's voices trailed off. They touched the cross and said goodbye to their papa. Yes, it was well over a year since he had died, but this scene still filled Clara's throat with emotion. After forcing it down with several hard swallows, she told the children to come along and wash up so they could cook supper.

As they walked through the grass that needed cutting one last time before frost, Clara prayed to God to help her through the next year like He had helped her through this one. He answered with His living presence, in the chickens scratching around the henhouse, in the cow grazing in the pasture, in the waning garden that needed to be plowed under soon. He had met her needs and more since Abram had died. Now He would meet her needs with courting Vernon, so she could decide if he would be a suitable husband for her and a suitable father for Edna and John.

Unfortunately, no matter how hard Clara prayed for Vernon to be those things, whether during the day or at night, when she woke in tears because she missed Abram, she never felt the same calm assurance she felt when she prayed about other things.

Maybe this part of her life was a test of faith. She had surely failed her faith when she had crawled into Jonah's lap and allowed him to comfort her as if she were a child.

In the kitchen, she and the children washed their hands. While they made a chicken casserole, rolls, green peas, and a blueberry cobbler with berries Vernon had bought from the grocery in South Boston, doubt crept into Clara's mind.

Where was her life taking her? She felt like a leaf in the wind: dried and brittle, about to be crushed under the weight of her coming choices, plus the desire to be a good mother to her children by finding them a father.

If only love could be found in that choice, but it wasn't meant to be.

Readers: please enjoy the first chapter of *The Colors of Eliza Gray.*

Holmes County, Ohio

Of all the times the boy across the table had mocked Eliza, she had never wanted to hurt him.

He was sneaky about it too. He would stop eating, make sure no one was looking, cover his ears, roll his eyes, and go back to his food, smirking.

But this was different.

He had elbowed his fork to the floor, crawled under the table, shoved his hand up her dress to her thigh, and had scrambled back to his chair before she could make sense of what had happened.

She probably could hurt him now, and she didn't even care about the beginning of a beard on his chin.

At the other end of the table, Mama and Papa spoke silent words to the boy's mama and papa. To Eliza's left, Tess and Ethan ate roasted chicken and cabbage soup. Beside the mocking boy, his younger brother drank milk.

Eliza tilted her head to one side. Three black bonnets and two wide-brimmed straw hats hung on pegs by the door. If someone made the mocking boy wear a white kapp, one of the bonnets, a white apron, and a black dress, he might understand how it felt to be her.

She straightened her head. No, that wouldn't work. Not unless he'd lost his hearing as a child. Time to think about something sweet and precious instead of him.

Behind Mama, in one of the boy's old cribs, Ivy pushed her lips in and out as if she were nursing. Similar to the color of Papa's beard, dark red hair covered her head. Ethan and Tess shared the same hair color, but Mama's hair gleamed in shiny black waves down to her waist when, at bedtime, she removed the white kapp and unpinned her hair. Compared to the women on the magazines at the store in town, Mama was as beautiful as they were. Eliza could've been her sister, except a younger, taller version, with a slender waist, black instead of green eyes, and a sharp nose instead of an upturned one. Mama also had crow's feet, a hint of gray at her temples, and a few wrinkles on her forehead from furrowing her brow. That's what she got for being mean. So much for thinking about something sweet and precious.

Across the table, the boy darted his dark eyes around in preparation for more mocking. Eliza drew her feet back and lowered her head to watch for the fork.

During these meals, when his mocking had

begun, back when she was a little girl with curls to her shoulders, she lowered her head to hide like a meek little rabbit in its den of briars, except her den of briars was a kapp sewn from stiff, white cloth. Tears in bed followed. They sometimes followed now, but not as often. Teary nights were never good, when she wished someone would place her in a wooden box and lower her into a hole in the ground.

She counted time in several hesitant breaths. No fork fell, so she raised her head. The boy elbowed his younger brother, who touched one ear and went back to his apple pie.

Being unable to hear meant Eliza had to study people's actions to understand what they meant. In this case, since the boy had only touched one ear, he didn't like mocking her. Eliza managed a smile. Unless he loved apple pie as much as Ethan loved apple pie.

Tess placed a slice before Eliza. Ignoring the mocking boy, she enjoyed the tart apples and flaky crust, washed down with cold swallows of milk.

Plate and glass empty, she leaned back against the wooden chair's hard slats.

The few words she could remember from long ago, "tree, water, and river," sometimes peeked above the nest of her memories like baby birds stretching their necks for a worm. No matter how hard she tried, no more words revealed themselves, as if the mama bird had pushed them from the nest.

The idea made her teary, but she'd rather do that later in bed.

When she tried saying those words now, people looked at her with widened eyes before turning away, which is why she'd stopped trying to speak as a child. She was grown now, as tall as the adults, and she hated it when they treated her like this. Even worse was when children and older boys and girls treated her like this.

Then there was the boy across the table. One day she'd prove she was no meek little rabbit, and he wouldn't dare touch or mock her again.

Plates cleaned, glasses emptied, the adults exchanged waves on the porch. The boy's mama and papa even included Eliza, giving her a warm feeling in her chest. As they went inside, her family left for the dirt road that led toward home.

The late autumn sun pressed searing rays into the land. On one side of the road, stalks of corn—green at the bottom, dusky brown at the top—filled a huge field. No breeze stirred the slender leaves nor the golden tassels hanging from the plump ears. On the other side of the road, heat waves hovered a shimmering mirage over a pasture, blurring a brown and white milk cow cropping grass in the shade of an oak. The aroma of manure and dark, rich earth filled the air, intensified by the heat.

Eliza lagged behind her family, preferring to walk by herself. What chores would Mama have for her this afternoon? Pump water from the well and tote it inside? Hoe the withering weeds in the garden? Peel potatoes for—

A hot breeze blew against the nape of her neck, carrying the sour warning that someone was behind her. She turned to peek from beneath the black bonnet.

And there they were, the two boys chasing the meek little rabbit. They carried fishing poles over their shoulders, so maybe they just wanted to see what was biting in the river.

She turned around. No, the oldest boy probably wanted to mock her again instead of fishing—or worse.

Eliza increased her stride to catch her family. Their shoes puffed dust into the air, now dry and still. The sun bore down on their black clothing. Sweat smudged shirts and dresses, darkened underarms and collars.

The oppressive heat surrounded her, concentrated beneath her black bonnet, settled into the hollow between her shoulder blades.

Something lifted her dress. She looked back in time to see the oldest boy jerk his fishing pole away, a grinning smirk twisting his face.

She felt teary again, like the little girl from long ago.

A flash of light caught her eye. To the right, beyond the rolling hills behind her home, the black belly of a cloud bulged and wallowed like a hog covered with mud.

A storm coming.

A cool gust of wind blew the ties of the bonnet around her face. Lightning flashed again, and she turned to see the boys running home, leaving a trail of dust in their wake.

She never expected the boy to touch her leg or raise her dress, but she should have.

Although she resembled Mama, when Papa shopped in town, she compared her reflection in a sunglass display mirror to the women on those magazines too. Yes, she looked as nice as they did. Young men in the area certainly thought so, because she drew their glances like an apple drew a horse. Regardless, even though the brushes and paste that Papa took home had brightened her teeth, no young man ever approached her with kindness in his eyes.

In the road ahead, another gust of wind swirled dirt and wisps of dried grass. Papa clamped his hand to his hat and walked faster. Beside him, Mama lowered her head over Ivy. Behind Mama,

Tess hurried along, black dress swirling about her ankles. Between Tess and Eliza, holding his hat to his head with both hands, Ethan took long, stilted strides. Papa needed to give him a haircut soon. Why would a man or boy want his hair to look like a bowl turned upside-down? The men in the magazines at the store were quite handsome, with thick hair cut either close or curly. How might it be to finger a man's curly hair, especially if it were brown like soil in the garden?

Papa and Mama turned toward the two-story white house, Tess and Ethan close behind. Knees rose and fell. Pants legs and dresses flapped in the wind. Eliza imagined a family of crows in a pasture, all rising and falling and flapping after a grasshopper, whose veined wings fluttered for its life.

From the swirling clouds, lightning flicked a snake's tongue, forked and brilliant, into the trees hiding the river. Papa broke into a trot. The trees swayed and bowed with the wind. Eliza wiped a huge warm raindrop from her cheek. In the dirt road leading to the house, more raindrops fell, evidenced by puffs of dust. The gray aroma of water filled the cooling air.

Everyone piled onto the porch to wipe their shoes on the mat at the door and enter one by one. Papa removed his straw hat to hang on one of the pegs by the door, followed by Ethan. Mama did the same with her black bonnet. Tess climbed the stairs and Eliza followed.

In the dark corner at the far end of their room, she sat on her bed. Shoes, black stockings, bonnet, and apron put away, she sat again to place her hand on the cool window. Huge raindrops struck the glass, sharing tiny kisses with her palm. The grass in the back yard swirled as if caught in the grip of Mama's spoon stirring cake batter. From the swollen clouds, lightning slashed the sky again and again.

Eliza waited. It always came. Always. Like one violent beat of her heart, a huge vibration buffeted her chest, then faded into gentle caresses.

She imagined a gentle man—not some cruel boy who mocked her because she couldn't hear—holding his hand to her heart—a man who enjoyed the outdoors, long walks beneath the trees, and nothing more than the simple pleasure of being together.

Across the room, Tess lit a lamp. Black smoke fluttered sooty fingertips toward the low, plank ceiling. She lowered the wick and replaced the glass chimney, lay her head on the pillow and opened a book from the nightstand.

Eliza took her hand from the window. She needed more paper for her projects. Maybe Papa would visit a store soon, and she could buy some with the few coins that Mama let her keep from making baskets.

First things first: allow the storm to end and gather mud at the river.

If that mocking boy left her alone.

Lightning flashed again, illuminating the rusted well pump at the end of the backyard, beyond the barn and chicken coop to the right, and the woodshed and basketmaking shop to the left.

Eliza reached into her mind for the first page of her memories, when Mama had slapped her as child because she only knew to get water from the river instead of the well. Chin trembling, Eliza had nodded as a single tear rolled down the four streaks of pain burning her cheek. A confused child did not deserve such treatment. If she ever found a way to tell Mama how deep the scars of that day had cut into her heart, she would.

Shaking the memory from her mind, Eliza went to the back porch. The final drops of rain were trailing from the sky in silver sprinkles of light. The trees stood tall as the wind died. She ran through the cool, wet grass toward the barn for an old bucket. Found in the hay loft seasons ago, it made the perfect container for gathering leaves, berries, mud, or any other color a project required.

Along the path to the river, the earthy aroma of

mold greeted her as she purposefully shuffled through last fall's wet leaves with her bare feet. In the branches, where green leaves were turning orange, red, and gold, a gray squirrel sat up while nibbling an acorn, furred tail curled over its back. Further on, to the side of the path, a partially eaten ear of corn marked a raccoon's supper, taken from the garden last night. Droplets of green-smelling water fell from the leaves, almost like daytime lightning bugs with crystalline beacons flashing, gathering, and dispersing the sunshine pouring from the clearing sky.

Eliza stopped at the river. The rolling water, tinted green from the leaves overhead, reflected swirls of sunlight sparkling into her eyes.

Around the bend to the left, the end of the boy's rowboat barely stuck out. He was probably at home, disappointed because he wasn't here to mock her.

Eliza left the bucket on the bank and gathered her dress to her knees. The current, slow and steady, kissed bare legs with cool lips. Raising the dress higher, she continued into the water to mid-thigh. Toes wiggling in the mud, eyes closed, she breathed in the spicy aroma of the leaves yet to fall in the woods behind her. The current swirled. She slipped in the mud, almost fell, and stepped back to ankle deep.

Something brushed her calf. Not looking, she swatted the fly away. It lit again and she swatted again. It lit on her thigh between her legs. She looked down to swat it accurately and realized the fly was the tip of the mocking boy's fishing pole, rising to touch where he shouldn't.

She whirled around. He dropped the pole and elbowed his younger brother beside him, then reared back and laughed like a rooster announcing sunrise. The younger brother took a step backward, fear in his widening eyes.

The time for tears was over.

Holding the dress up with one hand, Eliza went to the boy and jerked his hand to her thigh. He squeezed it, slowly licked his lips, and turned to wave his brother away, who ran into the path. The mocking boy faced Eliza again.

His dark eyes denied the shame of his brother's judgement, the desire to take instead of give, the willingness to hurt instead of understand. Swirling within the flecks of green around the black centers, which reflected her face and the river she loved so well, those things revealed something worse than mocking.

Yes, she could hurt him now.

She placed her hands on his shoulders, leaned in as if to kiss him, and drove her knee into his crotch. He grabbed his belly and fell on his side in the mud.

She kicked him to his back and clenched her fist. Not his mouth. Why cut her knuckles on his teeth? She drew back her hand, tightened the work-hardened muscles in her shoulder, bicep, and forearm, and with every ounce of strength she could manage, drove her fist into his nose, resulting in a spectacular gush of blood from his nostrils.

She leaned over the boy to wait for his attention. His eyes opened and he jerked away. Blood ran down his chin and neck and into his collar, similar to a male hummingbird hovering near a honeysuckle bloom. Tears squeezed from his eyes, closed again, but that wasn't enough.

Eliza sucked in air until her lungs ached and screamed into his face, demanding that he never bother her again.

She stepped over him as he continued to grimace in pain. He wouldn't dare tell anyone what she'd done. Other boys would mock him like he'd mocked her, so his explanation to his family had better be an interesting one when he finally limped his bleeding self home. Still, now that she'd hurt him, he might hurt her back. Whatever he might plan, she'd be ready.

She grabbed the bucket's wire handle and left for home.

No man nearby would ever care for her, but one somewhere else might. Did he live in town? Far away? Was he sitting by a lake or a river?

Doubt replaced hope, making her teary. Like her, even if he existed, he might know sadness and heartache as well.

Smiling up at the sunshine in the leaves, she wiped her eyes. The only way to find out was to meet him.

Readers: please enjoy the first chapter of *The Essence of Emmaline Strong*.

The Blue Ridge Mountains of Virginia haven't always been a problem for me. In my Jeep 4x4 this morning, driving along its curvy roads, the sheer drop-offs to one side or the other tweaking my vertigo, I realized how I was only one turn away from oblivion.

Life's like that. There's no denying it, so why even try? It's not like I'm special enough to dodge oblivion.

Oblivion.

What a word.

The drive passed quickly—well, *too* quickly—and I arrived at the one place in the world I did *not* want to be. After all, who would want a follow-up appointment with a doctor of any kind, let alone an eye specialist after a zillion or so tests, plus one they took blood for and I forgot to ask why, being as nervous as a long-tailed cat in a room full of rocking chairs, a cow with a buck-toothed calf, or any one of a million other sayings like those we have in the south. At least my sense of humor hadn't totally left me, but it wasn't far from it.

In the waiting room, as I prayed over and over

for my problem to not be what the specialist thought it was, a surreal feeling washes over me, as if my invisible words were bouncing off the ceiling and flying back at me, like my faith was a rubber ball and the ceiling was concrete. Considering everything I'd been through in the past two years—or in other words, chances at oblivion—I wouldn't be surprised. Still, I have a lot to be grateful for, but if this appointment went wrong, I might pull an epic wino drunk that would seriously upset my minister dad.

The vinyl chair squeaked when I crossed my blue jean-clad legs for the umpteenth time. I gave up and went to the single window overlooking the parking lot and imagined my town of Sufferer's Valley, tucked in mountains, and hoped it and my four-room house were firmly embedded in my mind's eye. That included my two five-string banjos, my acoustic guitar, and my last major purchase on plastic: a fine resonator guitar with flame-maple top, back, and sides, an ebony fretboard inlayed with mother of pearl diamonds, and a huge sound that blew me away the first time I played it.

Over two years ago, when I felt my life beginning to change in some horrible way, I either listened to or imagined the music and lyrics from some of my favorite musicians. Tony Rice would sing *Early Morning Rain, Song for a Winter's Night,* or play *Shenandoah* on his guitar, a 1935 Martin D-28, and my heart would slow from its runaway hammering deep inside my chest. More often than not, those wonderful melodies would do the trick. If not, Alison Krauss would sing *When You Say Nothing at all, Away Down the River,* or *Baby, Now That I've Found You,* and tears of joy would soothe me down to the marrow in my bones. For a newer member of the bluegrass movement, especially on the mandolin, I could always depend on Sierra Hull to send the blood roaring through my veins with the utter magic of her amazing touch on those eight strings, strung along such a small instrument, not to mention using her pure voice on tunes such as *Someone Like You, Summer's End,* and *Beautifully Out of Place.* Oh, and I can't forget Jerry Douglas playing *Hymn of Ordinary Motion* on one of his Beard resonator guitars, also known as a dobro. In my opinion, for the purest and sweetest tones that send me drifting away from life's troubles, it's hard to beat Jerry.

Yes, at this point in my life, I preferred slower, more poignant songs from those amazing artists. Given my situation, it made sense.

Shaking my head, I started to pray to be able to play my *own* instruments if the worst happened, but a door creaked open behind me. "Jordan, hon," the receptionist said, with her soft southern drawl, "you can come on back now." Another thing about the south: once you're on a first name basis with someone, mostly women, they add either "hon" or "sweetie" to the mix.

In the examination room, the doctor looked up from a notepad. "Hi, Jordan. Have a nice drive here this morning? The Blue Ridge certainly looks blue, doesn't it?"

I started to sit in the examination chair, but the doctor motioned me toward a normal chair next to the wall. I sat, and he rolled his chair closer. "Is your dad in the waiting room?"

Clamping my eyes shut, I swallowed. He would ask about Dad for one reason and one reason only. My heart jumped in my chest. I could hardly breathe. Before I realized I was crying, hot tears tracked down my cheeks.

"Jordan, is he here? Maybe your brother?"

I took a tissue from my purse and dabbed my eyes. "Is it Best disease?"

"I'm afraid the genetic testing confirmed it."

So that was why they took my blood. How did I miss that when I'd spent an entire day on my PC researching my possible condition? So, I was going blind, and worse than that, no cure—not a single one—existed.

I looked up at the yellow tile ceiling, trying to pretend it wasn't there, trying to pretend blue skies filled the stuffy examination room, trying to pretend I was standing in the chilly pool beneath the waterfall up the mountain behind my house. Even if I were there, my prayers would bounce off those blue skies and slap me in the face.

Then again, my mom, God rest her soul, would have a thing or two to say about my situation:

Well, sweety, you just have to take it in stride and trust God. Besides, I'll be around to help you get through it.

No, Mom, I'd say. How can you be around when you died giving birth to Teddy? And you weren't there when I caught Tyler, that lying SOB, cheating on me in college either.

It's time to get over that, you know. Another fella will come 'round before you know it.

What guy would want a blind woman, Mom? I'll be stuck in my house at the base of Sufferer's Mountain. I won't be able to drive. I won't be able to teach my students to play banjo, guitar, or resonator guitar. I won't be able to get my groceries.

I'll shrivel up and die, and the worst thing is how I won't have anyone to love. But hey, your life insurance came in handy when Dad helped me build that four-room shack I've got. See how much I've got to be grateful for? What's going blind compared to all that?

"Jordan, I know this is difficult."

I snapped out of my trance to face the doctor. "I think it's a little worse than difficult."

"You do have options, like special glasses. Gene therapy is promising, although it's a ways off yet. The best thing is to know what to expect. I'll tell you exactly that so it won't be too frightening."

The doctor went on to tell me how Best disease, also known as Best Vitelliform Dystrophy, was a type of juvenile macular degeneration. Then he said the one thing that completely made my day. "I'm not sure if you know this, but you should. It's inherited and can be passed on to children."

I bit my lower lip until the metallic taste of blood made me stop. I'd inherited this crap and shouldn't risk having children who might go blind like me. Just freakin' great, the final nail in the coffin, where my last threads of faith were laid to rest. First Mom, then Tyler, and now this, each a hammer banging those nails and me to my knees, where I'd never, ever, as long as I lived, pray again.

I stuffed the tissue in my purse and faced the doctor. "I read on the internet that it's degenerative. How long do I have before I can't do anything for myself?"

"It's usually diagnosed in younger people," he said, crossing his arms. "Yours is already advanced. I'd say under five years, but it could be more or it could be less. Would you like to make an appointment to talk about your options?"

I hated to be rude, but I went straight to the receptionist, asked her to send me the bill, and sped with squealing tires around the mountain curves to Sufferer's Valley and its only grocery store—for six bottles of the cheapest wine I could afford.

At home, I drank one each for the next six nights. Following *that* bit of wisdom, between brief phone calls from Dad, when I told him what had happened and how I was fine, I did the same thing for six more nights, until I finally saw the light, so to speak, like the country song Hank Williams recorded back in 1948.

The light I saw? Waking up in pee-soaked jeans and a puke-soaked blouse that smelled of sour grapes was *not* fun.

Showered and dressed in clean jeans and a red-flannel shirt, I went to my music room and took my favorite picture of Mom from the table by the window, where the sun could highlight her blonde hair. When my brother, Josh, and I were kids, he teased me about how he'd inherited her hair and I'd inherited my mousy brown mess from Dad. Good thing I didn't get Dad's banjo-neck physique, thin as the proverbial rail, but I did inherit Mom's hourglass figure. Also like Mom, although I'm not crazy about it, I inherited her five-two height. Oh, well, it sucks to be me at times. Big duh.

Because of how I'd acted at the specialist's office, and my resulting sloppy drunkenness, Mom would kick my behind if she were here, and she'd have a durn good reason.

From the time I was about ten until I left home for college, I played banjo at a local gathering spot in town. I was twenty and had come home from college for the weekend when Dad took the picture. Mom and Josh were dancing, both grinning like maniacs, her blonde hair shining in the fluorescent lights. Her baby bump, which would've been Teddy, bulged like she carried quintuplets, and I was grinning too.

I put the picture back.

Did I get Best disease from Mom or Dad? Dad was safe because of his age, but Josh, being two years younger than me and likely wanting to marry and have kids one day, should be genetically tested.

On my PC, I entered a social networking site that Dad frequented for church news. The green icon said he was online, so I sent a message asking if he knew about Best disease being genetic. He responded that he did, adding how Josh was tested negative for the gene a few days after I told them about my diagnosis.

Dad began typing another message, and I logged off the site. Lucky Josh, no worrying about passing on this nightmare to potential children. I clicked the PC to sleep, stood by the window, and there it was, the haze in my central vision.

My research said most patient's sight gradually deteriorated to 20-100, with 20-40 on the lower extreme and 20-200 on the upper end, what the medical community considered legally blind. The strangest part was how peripheral vision wasn't affected, but what good was that without central vision? Since the specialist had said the time to maximum sight loss was unknown, I'd head this crap off at the pass as much as I could, meaning I needed to make plans.

On the floor, I set my banjo case down, opened it, and ran my fingertips over the tailpiece, where the strings attach at the bottom, followed them all the way to the fifth string tuner for the shortest string, and kept going until I reached the four tuners on the peghead at the top of the neck. The feel of string and metal and wood was as familiar as my own body during a shower. Since I could shower with my eyes closed, I bet I could change strings on my banjo, dobro, and guitar with my eyes closed too.

With that problem conquered, what about teaching my students? I closed the banjo case, snapped the latches, and set it on its side. I could have them bring a digital recorder to record our lessons. Huh, about time something went my way.

I returned to the window. What about driving? Well, Dad would offer to chauffer my disabled self to the grocery store. The price I'd pay would be his caring suggestion to attend church, but that was better than starving to death.

Outside the window, beyond my backyard, the sloped beginning of Sufferer's Mountain rose over 2000 feet into the hazy clouds tinted with blue. Late October in the Blue Ridge. Oak, maple, and hickory trees on fire with red, orange, gold and every shade between. Unfortunately, my time to enjoy them was limited.

In my back jeans pocket, my phone played Dad's

tone, the melody to *The Sweet Bye and Bye*. Oh sure, *now* my phone worked. The signal usually sucked because of the mountains, so why couldn't it suck now?

I swiped the screen. "What's up?"

"Hi, honey. I tried to catch you on the PC a minute ago but you logged off. What's the chance you can play banjo for my service at the nursing home in the morning? The folks would love to hear you."

Pinching the bridge of my nose, I considered his request. Sure, the folks there liked my playing, and I liked playing for them. "I'll be there at 9:30."

"Want to ride with me?"

"I can still drive."

"What about church? It's been a while since you've been, you know."

"My banjo needs new strings. I'll hear you at the nursing home anyway."

"It's not the same. You've got all night to—"

"Breakfast in the morning."

"Doesn't take long."

"I'll sleep late."

"That's no better?"

I said nothing. I shouldn't have mentioned my sleep problems the last time we spoke.

"Maybe you should see a doctor about—"

"See you in the morning." I started to jab the end-call icon, but Dad said something I didn't catch. "What's that?"

"I said Josh will be in."

"I hope you two don't plan to gang up on me about my condition."

"He wants to. I told him to leave you alone."

"Tell him to pray about it." Durn, my faithless attitude in action. Besides, if my brother had driven all the way from the University of Virginia to visit, maybe I could get a few laughs out of him. He did that plenty when I broke up with the jerk in college, and finding humor where none existed pleased me to no end. Too bad I didn't have someone full-time to do that.

"You there, honey?"

"He could come with you to the nursing home."

"He's going out with friends tonight. Knowing him, he'll sleep in." Dad paused. "I thought I'd lost you."

Talk about double-meaning, as in the religious context of "being lost," which probably worried him concerning little old going-blind me. Still, I shouldn't have tried to end the call before he said goodbye. "I'll see him or I won't," I said. "Is he going back to school after church?"

"He mentioned it."

"That's the best I can do."

"How about coming for lunch around one? I haven't seen you in two weeks."

I waited for the rest. *And you only live on the other side of town.* I wanted to ask why he hadn't stopped by, but he'd likely been visiting "the sick and the shut-ins," practicing with the choir, holding Wednesday night Bible study and writing sermons. I told him I had some banjo lessons to plan for Monday and stuck the phone back in my jeans.

In the kitchen, I poured white wine for a change and raised the glass. "Here's to you, Josh. I'm sincerely happy you can continue our lineage without being afraid your children will go blind."

I sipped. "Maybe your future wife will have a brother who doesn't mind having a blind wife." I downed the semi-sweet liquid in one huge gulp. "Who doesn't mind if she shouldn't have kids either."

After an early dinner of a ham sandwich and tomato soup from a can, including another glass of wine, I channel-surfed until rain pattered against the living room window. In the music room again, I went to the window. The reddening leaves on the maple in the backyard trembled with a slight breeze. Midway up the mountain, barely illuminated by the dimming twilight, the breeze bent the fog to its will.

Like blindness was bending my life to *its* will.

Maybe tomorrow would start clear, with a gorgeous sunrise over the peaks to the east. I needed light to lift me, a beautiful red dawn to send my sadness scampering away like a kitten I once had.

I went back to the living room, plopped to the sofa, and thumbed the remote.

Huh. Not with *my* luck.

ABOUT THE AUTHOR

J. Willis Sanders lives in southern Virginia, with his wife and several stringed musical instruments.

With fourteen novels completed and more on the way, he enjoys crafting intriguing characters with equally intriguing conflicts to overcome. He also loves the natural world and, more often than not, his stories include those settings. Most also utilize intense love relationships and layered themes.

His first idea for a novel is a ghostly World War II era historical that takes place mostly in the midwestern United States, which utilizes some little-known facts about German POW camps there at the time. It's the first of a three-book series, in which characters from the first continue their lives.

Although he loves history, he has written several contemporary novels as well, and some include interesting paranormal twists, both with and without religious themes.

He also loves the Outer Banks of North Carolina, and he has written three novels within different time frames based on the area, what he calls his Outer Banks of North Carolina Series. As of

January 2023, he's writing another novel about the area.

And yes, he enjoys learning about the variations of Amish culture, which inspired his Eliza Gray and Clara Engelman series.

Other hobbies include reading (of course), vegetable gardening, playing music with friends, and songwriting, some of which are in a few of his novels.

To follow his work, visit any of these websites:

https://jwillissanders.wixsite.com/writer

https://www.facebook.com/J-Willis-Sanders-874367072622901

https://www.amazon.com/J-Willis-Sanders/e/B092RZG6MC?ref_=dbs_p_ebk_r00_abau_000000

Readers: to help those considering a purchase, please leave a review on Amazon.com, Goodreads.com, or wherever you bought this book. They help authors more than you may realize.

9 781954 763517